Praise for the Tales of the Captain Duke

"There are few words I can use to describe the emotional rollercoaster the second book has put me through, but dammit I would do it again!"

– Katherine Wunder (Amazon.ca)

"This was a really fun read [...] it is well written and keeps you engaged with its witty dialogue, fast paced story progression and charming character development."

– Aleksa Stefanovic (Goodreads)

"WAITING FOR THE NEXT BOOK..."

– Bernice Gowan (Amazon.com)

"This series is a great place for anyone to start as Diem charmingly reinvents piratical history with airships, and challenges gender roles and diversity. This is a lighthearted adventure that isn't afraid to get serious from time to time."

– Wendy (BiblioSanctum)

"Imaginative and Captivating. I couldn't put it down. Diem has a unique yet cohesive style of writing."

– Joey Methé (Amazon.ca)

Also by Rebecca Diem:

Tales of the Captain Duke

The Stowaway Debutante

From Haven to Hell

A Gentleman and a Scholar

Of Tempests and Teacups *(coming 2017)*

Tales of the Captain Duke

A Gentleman and a Scholar

Rebecca Diem

Eliana,
Everyone has a story!
R. Diem

WOOLF LIKE ME
Publishing

Cover art by Sarah Dier-McComb
Cover design by Steve Armstrong

First Edition

Woolf Like Me Publishing
ISBN: 978-0-9938874-7-5

For my siblings, Andrew, Sarah, and Leah

143

Table of Contents

Chapter 1: In which our heroine receives an unexpected guest

The tallport was busy with activity as the airships flew in to dock for the evening. Leisurecraft of pale, polished wood and speedy brass flyers, all flying the Tradist colours. They filled the spokes of the tallport, a simple two-tiered structure nestled in the clearing. The crews disembarked and greeted each other, boasting of their latest haul as they unloaded their cargo from hidden compartments in the hull and into an elevator to be lowered to the ground below. Teams of pilots were busy sorting and packing the goods under the watchful eye of Cat, standing on a crate and shouting her orders to be heard above the fray.

Clara observed the scene from her post at the top of the central tower of the new tallport they had installed to accommodate all the additional aircraft. Her attention commanded by the intricate dance of coordinating the activities of a dozen separate pirate crews, directing the flow of goods and marking down the shipment details to be transcribed later into the inventory books. She shaded her eyes against the fading light as she watched the final airship approach. It loomed large on the horizon, its hull now bearing the unfamiliar moniker *Eye of Iris*, but to Clara, it was home.

"Miss Clara?"

She turned to find Madge waiting with an overflowing receipt book in hand.

"You've filled another book already? How many ships today?"

"Three dozen." The short pilot tucked her curly hair behind her ear and beamed with pride, "Easy pickings today. The word is spreading about the inspections. To be honest, I think we're doing the Tradists a favour keeping these captains on their toes. And the best part is they always 'donate' the top shelf stock for quality control."

"Excellent. Madge, you're a natural. Take this book down to Cat and then help Peg with the inventory. We'll be ready to take another shipment to Keswick tomorrow."

The pirate saluted, and Clara did her best to keep a straight face. She wasn't an officer, but the crew had taken to treating her as such since she was put in charge of organizing their new scheme. The last major raid had gone sour after one of their own betrayed them. Their return to the pirates' hideout had only brought more troubles, when their former officer, Robbie, staged a mutiny, pitting friends and allies against one another before flying an airship laden with gunpowder straight into the Haven. The very airship they had found her on after she'd turned stowaway while running away from her engagement party that summer. Robbie survived. Others did not.

They had lost good pilots that day, and the crew mourned their loss. Much had changed in the weeks since the attack, but they had rallied together, steadfast in their dedication to the Captain Duke and his philosophy of 'liberating' the cargo of the Tradists for the benefit of all. But the Captain… Well, he had other important matters to care for.

It had been Clara's idea to break the pirates into smaller groups and pretend to be inspectors for the Tradist shipments. They funnelled the stolen goods into a black market network of merchants through Master Tims to avoid the high tariffs of the Association of Merchant Traders that had formed after the dissolution of the East India Company. Here, on an island at the centre of the Derwentwater, in the bucolic Lake District, they undermined everything the Tradists stood for. A small team, working together to spread the wealth.

Looking over the bounty before her as it was loaded into the elevators, Clara grinned at their success. At this rate, even with the setbacks they had encountered this season, they were on track to best last year's figures by the end of the month.

The largest airship was nearly at the dock, and Clara could now see the figures running about the deck. She waved at the tall woman standing at the prow, and walked along the spoke, waiting until the airship had been secured to send in the porters to help unload. Nessa crossed the rope bridge to stand with her as they supervised the work. Her long, blonde hair was tied back in a neat braid, ever a contrast to Clara's unruly brown curls, blowing wild in the cool September breeze.

"That was a long one. Did you have a pleasant trip?"

"A bounteous one. We covered most of the northeastern shore, turned back after Liverpool. We've a full hold. Had to stop to add the extra hydrogen buffers," replied Nessa. She handed over the logs and set her crew to their tasks before growing serious, reaching out to touch Clara's arm, "How is Trick?"

"The Captain is with him. He barely eats the food

before him," Clara sighed. "But the… it looks as though it's healing."

The two women stood in silence for a long moment before Nessa ventured to speak again.

"Your contacts at the university—have you heard back from your sources? Anything at all that could help him?"

"I sent a message, but there's been no reply. It's been three weeks and I'm afraid it was lost. That, or something is terribly wrong. I'm thinking—perhaps on the next run we'll go to Reading ourselves."

Clara realized she was wringing her hands—a nervous habit—and forced herself to unclench her fingers, smoothing the violet fabric of her overskirt and taking a deep breath.

Nessa frowned, staring into the distance.

"Clara, how many crews were sent out?"

"Eleven."

"And all are accounted for?"

"Yes, yours was the last to come in."

"Then who is that?"

Clara turned to look in the direction Nessa pointed. An odd, bulbous contraption was headed straight for the tallport, and it was not one of theirs. Clara signalled to the pilots on the docks and they gathered behind her and Nessa, waiting for the stranger to arrive. The aircraft sputtered and burped its way to a free spoke before a single pilot wearing a large pair of goggles threw out a tether and expertly moored his ship, leaping out onto the dock and walking towards them. Out of the corner of her eye, Clara saw Nessa reach for her pistol and put out a hand to stop her.

"Do you know him?" Nessa asked as the pilot removed his cap and goggles and shook out his tangled brown curls.

"Yes," said Clara. "He's my brother."

Chapter 2: In which our hero finds himself at his wits' end

The Captain Duke sat on a richly-patterned ottoman, arms crossed as he stared at the rapidly cooling bowl of stew on the table before him. He watched as the steam curled over the lip of the dish, then as it faded to nothing, the chunks of vegetable congealing in the broth. The bread—fresh baked that morning—had crusted over. It had been a favourite meal of Trick's, specially prepared by Peg now that she'd recovered from the attack on the Haven. And still his friend did nothing but stare out the window in silence.

At least he'd been able to move Trick to the armchair so he could feel the breeze from outside. He'd spent too long in his sickbed—and the Captain did not believe it healthy to go so long without fresh air, no matter what was practiced in the cities. They were pilots, they belonged to the sky. More than anything, he wanted to take Trick up on a run over the hills and valleys, somewhere he could see the landscape bending into the distance and feel the sharp autumn breeze run through his hair. But his friend, his mentor, was not yet recovered.

The Captain directed his rage at the tiny chunks of early carrots, floating in the broth. He nudged the table with the toe of his boot and watched the liquid slosh in the bowl. For a moment, Trick turned his gaze to the eddies in the stew. He raised his eyes to meet the Captain's, but his blank stare tore at the Captain Duke's heart. He could sit here no longer. He rose and left the room as Trick resumed the position he'd held since that terrible night: cradling the bandaged stump of his right arm.

The Captain walked through the halls of the southern wing until he reached the edge of the provisional repairs, and leaned against the empty doorframe. Beyond, his home lay in ashes.

There was some hope for its eventual restoration. Cat and Mouse had flown to Keswick for aid after figuring out the traitorous Robbie's plan, and by the looks of it, nearly every able-bodied soul had responded. He'd been overwhelmed by the flurry of activity after the explosion. He'd never forget the horror, watching the gunpowder-filled airship flying towards his home.

The firefighters had worked to douse the last of the flames while Mrs. Cottingham took charge of the recovery area, directing her staff in handing out blankets and bowls of warm soup. The town barber had set up an impromptu surgery by the airdocks and was helping Nurse Susan to treat the injured crewmembers. He never expected so many to come to their aid, and it steeled his heart against the tragedy of it all. They had buried the four fallen pilots in a grove on the southern end of the island. But that night, his focus had been on the living.

The Captain's chest grew tight at the memory of the goodwill, the community their cause had engendered. Master Tims had stood beside him as they watched the crew and villagers work together as a single unit. *We take care of our own*, Tims had replied when the Captain tried to thank him. The Captain Duke knew that the town tolerated their illicit activities, but had never expected that they would embrace them so wholly in their time of need. It gave him cause to hope that the future held a different path forward. He was tired of fighting alone.

The embers had still been smoking as he sat with the pilots, listening to Mouse tell the tale of how he and his sister had managed to fly his galleon with no crew, reaching Keswick in record time. He'd promised each of the young siblings a new set of pistols.

But then, Nessa had appeared by his side. In his distracted state, he hadn't noticed until she stood at his elbow.

"Captain?"

Her grave expression had demanded his full attention.

"What is it?"

"It's Trick. His arm…"

A lump had lodged in his throat as he followed her to the makeshift infirmary in a small tent by the port where a loud argument was underway. He was greeted by what might have been a humorous scene under better circumstances: Trick, standing in a corner and brandishing a small hammer, facing off against the butcher, who held a saw.

"I tell you, it is not happening. Find a different way. Captain, tell him."

He held his right arm close to his body.

The Captain Duke had swallowed hard before he could manage to speak,

"Trick, let me see it."

Reluctantly, breathing heavily through the pain, Trick

had uncovered his forearm and extended it for him to see the wound. The Captain Duke forced himself to look at the gruesome injury, even though he felt as though the air had been sucked out of his lungs. The bullet had been intended for him as Trick held the window open for their escape during the firefight with the mutineers. He wanted to rage, to fight, to do anything but crush the faint hope in Trick's eyes. Instead, he had summoned all his remaining courage.

"The bone is shattered, Trick. You know what that means as well as I do. Even if we set it, infection is certain."

"No."

"Trick, please," said Nessa, moving into the tent.

It was rare to witness the fearless piratess shed a tear, but the Captain Duke could see them rolling down her cheeks. He remembered wishing that he was permitted such a display of the emotion he felt at knowing that Trick would never again string the bow of his beloved violin. After a few long moments, Trick sat and accepted the bottle of whiskey passed to him. When he'd looked up at the two of them, his expression was one of utter defeat. His voice was gruff as he spoke.

"Will you stay?"

"Of course we will," said Nessa.

The Captain Duke had nodded. He had checked to ensure that the cloths were boiled and the instruments cleaned by fire and spirits before allowing the operation to proceed. Trick refused to be made insensible, but gripped a strap of leather in his teeth while the Captain and Nessa held him still. They stayed, for all of it.

Flesh might heal, but this wound ran deeper. Trick had

lost more than his arm; he'd lost some crucial piece of himself. In the days after the Incident, as the Captain Duke had taken to referring to Robbie's mutiny in his mind, it had quickly become apparent that Trick was not recovering. He was listless. He barely spoke, ate the barest minimum to survive. The Captain felt helpless. He was consumed by the need to bring back his friend. He could think of nothing else. The crew needed him, needed him to lead them into whatever uncertain future remained for them. But he could not do it without Trick.

It was Clara, though, who saved them. Always Clara.

He'd been standing at the base of the new tallport, watching the hubbub of construction as the pilots and villagers set to their new task with a renewed energy he could not feel. She had found him there, and stood with him for a long while before speaking.

"Captain?"

He'd turned to her, but he couldn't speak. She'd reached out her hand, and he'd taken it.

"Captain, I think I can help."

"There's nothing to be done now."

A small spark lit in his heart as she reached up and tucked his hair behind his ear. Somehow, without his knowing, he'd come to rely on her calm determination.

"Really, though. I know someone who may be able to help Trick."

"Who?"

After a half-second's hesitation, she'd answered.

"My brother."

"The scholar?"

"Yes."

"How so?"

"Well, he's a bit of a tinkerer. At the moment he's actually on a study exchange at Lovelace."

"The women's college?"

"The *university*," Clara had corrected him with a smile. "He wanted to study with Professor Sewell and she accepted him as an assistant."

"Sewell. The war profiteer."

"You mean the country's foremost expert in biomechanical manipulations. Let me write to him. He must have contacts there who will know how to help."

He took a deep breath, "What will you tell him? I doubt he's eager to come to the aid of pirates."

"I think we should try. I know he'll do the best he can. You saw how Keswick answered our call; maybe it's time to forge new alliances. There's still so much possibility. This isn't over, Captain. The crew, the village, Master Tims, we're all here."

The Captain had said nothing, but when he met her eyes he could see her concern. He thought better of arguing and instead pulled her into his arms. He liked how she fit against his body. The memory of the kiss they had shared on the beach the night of the Incident still lingered in his mind, bringing a smile whenever he allowed himself to dwell on it.

They hadn't yet had time to speak of it, but the small tokens of affection had continued: a touch on the arm, a smile as their eyes met when they shared a meal. One night he'd found her asleep in the study, exhausted from the hours she and Cat had spent salvaging what they could of the account books, copying the figures into fresh ledgers. Little Cat had woken immediately at his entrance, ever the pilot in training. She'd sleepily climbed the stair as he carried Clara to the room they both shared with Nessa now that the Bird's Nest in the upper gable had been lost to the explosion. The way that Clara curled her fingers into his hair made him yearn to wake her with a kiss. He'd tucked her into her bed, then left for his own after a murmured 'Good night,' sleepless, staring up at the tin-plated ceiling until the first rays of dawn.

Clara was a lady of good standing, pirate or no, and he held her honour dearer than his own. One day, soon, they would have time to talk. To fly out together over the hills. To give in to the joy they found in each other's company. But now, there were more pressing matters at hand.

The Captain Duke was still standing in the burnt frame, lost to daydreams, when Mouse called for him.

"Captain? Clara said to come and fetch you quick."

"What's happened?"

"Her brother is here!"

The Captain Duke followed the boy through the manor to the ballroom they now used as a gathering hall. As they passed a dusty window, he paused to brush the soot from his long, blue coat. His hair was tangled and he smoothed it back with impatient fingers, wishing he had more time to prepare. He felt nervous, meeting one of Clara's family for the first time. *He's here for Trick*, the Captain Duke reminded himself. But he straightened his posture, lifting his chin as he entered the room.

Clara was sitting on a sofa with a young man who could have been her twin—heart-shaped faces and identical dark brown curls, though his were cut short. The Captain was struck by their similarities as they both looked up at his entrance. Then, Clara rose and dashed across the room toward him, the long purple overskirt she favoured swirling around her legs, clad in slim black pants. She was smiling as she took him by the hand and led him into the room. She was radiant.

"Archie is here, Captain! Captain, this is my brother, Archie Whittington. Archie, I am pleased to present the Captain Duke."

The young man rose, extending a hand. He had a pleasant smile and a firm handshake.

"I've heard a few tales, but none that measure up to Clara's glowing commendations," said Archie.

The Captain wanted to ask a thousand questions—firstly, whether he could actually help Trick. Instead, he did his best to quell his worries, and smiled at their new guest.

"Welcome to the Haven."

Chapter 3: In which our heroine has high hopes

Clara was seated on a bench on one side of a long table they had salvaged from an old storage room, with her brother by her side. It was a simple dinner, as the kitchens were somewhat worse for wear—but Cook was able to work wonders with even the simple galleys on board the airships. Tonight was a hearty roast with early autumn vegetables. Cat and Mouse were across the table, enthralled by Archie's stories about his latest mechanical adventures and mishaps at the university.

"Imagine my surprise when the door opened—my quiet corner of study was, in fact, a powder room!" he exclaimed, eyes twinkling. "They have facilities for the male scholars, of course, but there's so few of us no one could be bothered to remember their location. Thankfully my peers took pity and permitted me to join their company. By the time I found the gentlemen's lounge, I was already accustomed to the engaging debates of the after-dinner parlours. In fact, I prefer them. Professor Sewell's laboratory is at the cutting edge of innovative discovery, filled with the brightest minds in the Empire."

Mouse was leaning so far forward, Clara thought he might tilt over into the potatoes, a forkful of beef forgotten in his hand.

"Is that where you built your craft? How did you get the balance on the rotors?" he asked.

"And what model did you use for the suspension? I've never seen such a set up," added Cat.

The two children had examined her brother's flying machine, but only after receiving his express permission. Clara thought he might regret it; the siblings had been near to disassembling the aircraft just to see if they could put it back together themselves. They likely could, she thought.

"Heavens, no. The Professor would murder me if I used her equipment for my little contraptions. I took a prototype glider I had started on the Isle and added a mechanical propulsion system using the Krebs method…"

The three of them carried on their conversation, lost in the art of cogs and gears. Clara was happy to listen, though the subject was of little interest to her despite years of participation in her brother's experiments. It was advantageous to have some basic knowledge of the mechanics of flight, but the details were of little concern to her as long as they kept the airship aloft. She sighed and tucked her hand under her chin. She missed her brother's boundless enthusiasm and infectious delight, even if the memories of past dinners in their family home gave rise to small eddies of grief. But, they were together again, and that itself was a matter of celebration.

Clara rose to retrieve a bottle of wine from the sideboard, and was startled as Archie rose beside her. The company stared, until the Captain Duke cleared his throat and rose at the head of the table. Suddenly, all the male pilots were standing sheepishly, even little Mouse. Clara realised, with complete dismay, that it was for her benefit. Blushing madly, she brought the wine round.

"Now that we are here together, might I propose a toast?"

Clara shot Nessa a look of gratitude as she and the rest of the women stood as well. The bottle was passed and glasses were filled. Clara turned to the Captain, but he merely nodded in her direction. Clara took a breath and straightened her shoulders.

"There's no doubt we've had a rough haul these past weeks. But I could not ask for a better crew to share these trials and tribulations with. Because of you, we're on track for our best season yet. We've made our way through the storm—and I'll not pretend there are clear skies ahead—but I can see marvels on the horizon."

She turned first to her brother, "To Archie; may the future yield to your innovations. I wish you luck and commend you for joining us in helping a dear friend."

Then she raised her glass to the head of the table: "...and to the Captain Duke, our leader through the good times and the bad, for bringing our enterprise together. May you ever find friends in your time of need."

"And to Clara," said the Captain, before she could finish, "for your courage and ingenuity. You've shone the light on a new path forward, and for that we are ever at your service."

Clara blushed again as the assembled pilots cheered. She could feel her brother's curious look, but took the Captain's compliment with pride. She had worked hard to earn her place in this crew, and she raised her voice along with theirs:

To the winds, to the clouds, to a life lived well,
Take me up to the sky!
To the heavens above and the land far below,
Pilot, keep to the sky!

To the sun on your face and the stars in your eyes,
Captain! Give me the sky!

She met the Captain's eye as they finished the toast, and smiled before drinking deeply.

After dinner, they retired to the library with Archie to fill in the details of their situation. Nessa and the Captain Duke interjected only when needed to elaborate on the messier details of Trick's circumstances. Clara could see how it pained them, and did her best to inject some optimism into the situation. After all, her brother had studied alongside the very best. Surely he could help Trick.

Archie paused in his note-taking to lean back in his chair.

"Well, it sounds like a simple enough case. We'll certainly be able to restore basic functionality to the subject."

"To Trick," said Nessa, eyes narrowing.

"Yes, of course," he replied quickly.

"Well, that's wonderful news," said Clara. "Isn't it, Captain? Trick will have the best treatment in the country. He'll get better now."

"I think we should pay our patient a visit first," the Captain said.

The lines of worry seemed permanently etched on his brow. Clara had a moment's thought of reaching up to smooth them away, entirely inappropriate in present company. But she laid a hand on his arm and he gave her a grateful look.

"Excellent idea. Shall we?"

She lifted the bag of Archie's tools from the settee and set off for the door.

"Oh, Clara, really. You mustn't exert yourself so," Archie called, intercepting her and retrieving his equipment. "Allow us," he said, handing the satchel to the Captain Duke.

She felt her temper rising. Clara turned on her heel and led the way from the room, but not before witnessing the smirk exchanged between the Captain and Nessa. Face burning, she guided their group upstairs to the room designated for Trick's convalescence. As she walked, Clara forced herself to take deep breaths. Archie was here to help, she reminded herself; this was for Trick.

By the time they reached his chambers, Clara was feeling far more forgiving about the situation. She knocked lightly on the door before calling out,

"Trick? There's company here to see you."

Nessa and the Captain Duke entered the room with her, while Archie hung back, allowing them space. Trick was sitting by the window, the room lit by a single lamp. The Captain Duke set about lighting more lamps and stoking the fire against the evening chill. Clara approached to sit in the chair across from him, reaching out to take his good hand. His eyes turned to her, but they held no emotion. It was as though he had been hollowed out from within. But, after a moment, he squeezed her hand back. Clara smiled,

"Trick, I'd like you to meet my brother, Archie. I think he might be able to help. Do you remember him from my stories? He put me on the airship you found me on, ball gown and all."

She caught a hint of a smile. It was a good sign. Clara waited until Trick nodded, then gestured to Archie to come forward.

"Archie, this is Patrick Kilarney, first officer to the Captain Duke. Trick, my brother, Lord Archibald Whittington. He is a scholar at Lovelace, and an assistant to Professor Georgina Jameson Sewell."

Archie's manner changed as he approached the injured man. His face was open, his expression sincere and respectful.

"It's an honour to meet you, sir. I am ever so grateful for your kindness towards my sister. Let me assure you," he said, kneeling. "I will do everything in my power to aid in your recovery. Everything. Now, may I see?"

It felt as though everyone in the room was holding their breath. It was a long, long moment as Archie knelt with a hand extended, patiently, expectantly, but radiating a sense of calm authority. Finally, Trick sought the Captain's eyes. Arms crossed, expression stern, he gave his affirmation, and Trick stretched out his injured limb. Clara let out a sigh of relief as she watched the care with which her brother examined her friend, asking questions in a quiet, professional manner, nodding as he received the barest response. He did not flinch at the sight of the injury, moving the limb this way and that, assessing the range of motion as Trick grew more comfortable. In whispers, he confessed his fears.

"Pardon, sir?" Archie asked.

"I can't—I don't think I'll be able to—it's hopeless, is it not?"

"Hardly, sir. I've seen many cases like yours at the

university. Some are worse off, some better. But all our patients have been able to recover some of their function — in several cases they have exceeded their original abilities. Professor Sewell's work is a wonder to behold. But first, we must make sure you're strong enough to endure the treatment. Your injury is healing well; the surgeon did fair work on this graft, though I would recommend a salve to aid in the process. I also have exercises we can work through to build up your strength again. Does that sound agreeable to you, sir?"

"Call me Trick," he said.

Clara smiled, and began to relax. Everything would be okay.

Chapter 4: In which our heroine addresses a matter of courtesy

A week later, nothing was okay.

ping* *ping *ping

Clara focused her aim and steadied her breath as she shot each bottle off the remnants of the wall in front of her. The corner of her mouth twisted into a smile as the fourth and fifth bottles shattered. But with the sixth, the bullet grazed the neck, tipping it over to lay there intact, mocking her. She resisted the urge to employ one of the curse words in her expanding vocabulary and gathered her focus once more. Clara raised the pistol and slowly squeezed the trigger—

"Clara!"

She let out her breath in a huff, "What?"

"Apologies, ma'am, the airships are returning," said Peg, standing in the doorframe of the Haven, arms akimbo.

Clara took a breath and shook her head, "Peg, I've told you. I'm not an officer. Please don't call me ma'am."

"Not *yet.* Best to get in your good books early. Especially considering your chosen methods of dealing with those who cross you," said Peg with a significant look at glass littering the ground.

"If only it was the real thing. Is there word?"

"Sighted near Manchester yesterday, headed south, but nothing since then. We have our contacts on the alert; we'll find Robbie eventually."

Clara felt her mouth tighten at the cursed name. The traitor had landed on the beach right before her eyes. He had started the mutiny. He had stabbed Anderssen, who died in her arms. He had set fire to the gunpowder ship, aimed it directly for their home. He had stood there, terrified, as she aimed her pistol for his heart. And Clara had let him get away. It did not matter what the crew thought or how many times the Captain Duke reassured her. She had allowed her own weakness to prevail. Clara said nothing, but turned back to her task. She pictured Robbie's head on each of the bottles. With a steady hand, she shot the last three clean through. She lifted her chin and turned back to Peg, holstering her weapon.

"There. I'm finished."

She kicked aside a piece of burnt molding, the layers of white ash sifting softly beneath her boots. Peg walked out from the main part of the manor, and put a hand on her shoulder.

"Clara, you mustn't blame yourself. I was half-dead and lying on the beach, useless to all. I might not have taken the shot either. Robbie's a master manipulator. And an explosion like that shocks your brain, it messes with your mind after."

"I just—I can't shake this feeling. He's out there. I had a chance to stop him, and I failed. We're still in danger because of me."

"No, we're in danger because Robbie Codswaddle

betrayed us. And he'll need time to recover, to regroup. He's impetuous and petty, but he is not a stupid man, and he was counting on more of us turning on the Captain Duke to follow him. He won't attack so soon, not since Nessa cast a black mark on his name at every airbour in the Empire."

Clara sighed, "I suppose you're right. And if anyone can root him out, it would be Ness."

"That's the spirit! And your aim is certainly top-notch. He ought to be quivering in his boots for the day he crosses your path again."

Clara surveyed the damage around her. They had worked hard to restore the central part of the manor, but the north wing was ruined beyond repair. It would need to be completely rebuilt, and there was no time before the storm season. They needed to find a solution, and soon.

Peg threw an arm around her in reassurance, "Look, you've certainly done more than your fair share of fixing. The crew has purpose again. We're bringing in a better haul than ever. And Trick is eating again! Real food. Hearty stuff."

"It's true," said the Captain Duke, appearing in the doorframe.

Clara noticed his reluctance to step beyond the threshold into the ruins. And yet, he often came to this spot to look upon the cremated remains of the Haven. So much had changed. There was little to be gained by staying, and yet, they stayed. There were times when she felt as though they were caught in a maelstrom, twisting and whirling in place with no way to see a path through to calmer skies. But, in spite of the weariness that showed around his eyes, the Captain was smiling.

"I swear I even heard him make a joke yesterday morn. I think those exercises your brother has him doing are making a real difference."

Clara rolled her eyes.

Peg lifted an eyebrow.

"Yes, Archie's a miracle-worker. Satisfied?" Clara huffed.

"I hate to remind you at such a delicate time, but it was your idea to bring him," the Captain smirked. "The crew is certainly enamoured."

It had been her idea, and Clara did not regret it, seeing the improvement in Trick's condition. But all week it had been the same. Archie pulling out a chair for her at the table. Archie intervening anytime she attempted to carry anything heavier than a pincushion. And it wasn't just him—the crew had begun to treat her differently. No more jostling at the bench for supper or teasing humour. They had reacted with surprise when she joined in the work unloading a large haul of shearling until she gave them a look that spoke to their imminent peril if they were to comment. Clara missed the camaraderie she had previously enjoyed.

"It's fine. I just hate to be treated with such… courtesy," she said, scowling.

"Oh, is that it?" Peg laughed, "Don't think we haven't noticed. You've the patience of a saint, ma'am, but you'll need to have a talk with dear Archie ere long."

"And what can I say? Apologies, dear brother, you're being far too polite?"

She narrowed her eyes as the Captain wisely stifled a chuckle.

Peg crossed her arms, "It's not the politeness. It's a matter of respect."

"My brother does respect me," she protested.

"It's a different matter, being respected as a lady. Not the same as being respected as yourself."

"It is different," echoed the Captain. "You earned the admiration and respect of the crew not by means of your name or sex, but through cleverness, hard work, determination. You've saved our lives over and again with your ideas."

Clara fought the blush that rose in her cheeks at such a compliment. She'd changed in the weeks since she'd flown away from the Isle of Wight and joined the crew of the Captain Duke.

"He's treating me like a debutante."

"And what will you do about it?" asked the Captain.

He hesitated, then stepped through the door, the ash puffing up in soft clouds around his dark boots. Clara hardly noticed Peg taking her leave as the Captain crossed the distance between them, heartbeat jumping as he stood close to her. And then they were alone. They had not yet discussed that kiss on the beach, but it was always at the forefront of her mind when she found herself near to him.

"You're outside," she said.

"We both are."

"But you never come out here."

"I'm here now," he said, casting his eyes around the ruins before meeting her gaze once more. "It's not as bad as I thought."

The stone foundation was streaked with soot and debris littered the ground. Only the hearth stood tall in the former kitchens, its chimney mostly intact.

"Captain—," she said, reaching for his hand.

"Trick is healing. He may finally be ready to move forward. Perhaps it's time for the rest of us to do so as well. I don't know what the future holds, but it's time we meet it. For me, it's letting go of this place.

"We could rebuild it, somewhen."

"One day," he agreed. "But we've been exposed here. The Haven is no more than a name now."

"We'll need a plan," she said, holstering her pistol.

He gave her a broad smile, "There's the piratess."

Clara was feeling like herself again. She reached up and tangled her fingers into his long red hair before rising on her toes to touch her lips to his. She wanted to see if it still felt like lightning, and her heart skipped as he welcomed her kiss. This was different from the night of the mutiny. This time felt like a slow, curling heat as the sensation spread throughout her body, and she pulled him closer. This time, she was patient, taking her time to savour the embrace, the feeling of his lips as they brushed against her own. The Captain wrapped his arms around her waist and held her against him as she rose to stand on her toes. They broke apart, but still she held on to him. She could feel his heartbeat twinned to her own, racing under the hand she held against his chest. Breathless, she met his eyes. There was a promise in them, and she felt his hands tighten about her hips before he regained his senses and took a deep breath.

"To the future," he said, at last.

Clara felt the blush on her cheeks, but she was determined to shake off any sensibilities that would foil her enjoyment of such a tantalizing moment. But for now, they had work to do.

"Come," she said, taking his arm. "Let's find Nessa and start plotting."

As they made their way through the manor together, Clara's mind was whirling between the matters at hand. The kiss—she had feelings for the Captain, there was no denying it. But there was the Haven to deal with, the question of where to move the crew and how, so many details to be worked out. And then, of course, the matter of Trick's recovery took obvious precedence over something so silly as a mere flirtation. But deep in her heart, she knew this was no simple crush. It needed the space and time to grow into whatever form it was meant to take. What would her family think if she ran off with a pirate captain? Although, she supposed she already had. She was a pirate herself now, after all, and a grown woman.

By the time they reached the entrance hall, Clara had worked out exactly how to bring up the issue of Archie's perception of her. She would simply explain to her brother that his behaviour was an impediment to her reputation amongst the crew and ask that he kindly desist. It was only a matter of explaining the context of his behaviour. They found him by the entryway, with Mouse at his side.

"Clara, Captain, how lovely. Mouse was about to show

me the grounds. Would you care to join us for a stroll?"

"Actually, we have a great deal of work to do. But if you have a moment—," she began, before Archie interrupted.

"Goodness, are those father's duelling pistols? Really, Clara, set them aside before you injure someone."

Clara's eyes narrowed. She briefly registered the Captain's muttered "Oh boy," as she marched over and twisted her brother's arm behind his back.

"Ow! Clara!" he yelled, mostly out of shock.

"Right. We're going to have a talk," she said, pushing him outside and slamming the door behind them.

Chapter 5: In which our hero finds a moment of peace

"They've been yelling for a while," said Mouse. He sounded impressed.

"Well, it sounds as though they have quite a lot to discuss," said the Captain Duke.

Cat rested her chin in her hands, "Brothers. Honestly."

"Hey!" shouted Mouse, but the Captain cleared his throat and they returned their attention to the scene outside the window.

Clara and her brother were doing battle on the front lawn, accentuating their various points of contention with emphatic gesticulation and raised voices. Clara crossed her arms and looked away as her brother made his plea, pointing toward the airship docks and to the ground he stood on. Then, Clara fixed a formidable glare upon her brother and stormed towards him. She stopped just short of the young man, forcing him to take a step back. Despite her smaller stature, she gave the impression of a far greater menace, and the Captain silently reminded himself to stay on her good side. Clara gave a wave of her hand encompassing all of the Haven, before turning with a hand to her head and walking away a few steps. Archie's shoulders turned inward. Defeated, he followed, resting a hand on her shoulder when she turned. He moved his hands to hold both of hers in supplication as he pleaded with her. The Captain could see her smile grow as she wiped away tears. Finally, Clara nodded and wrapped her brother in a hug as the siblings reached some sort of agreement. The Captain Duke and his fellow spies ducked behind the curtains as the two of them turned back to the Haven, arm in arm.

"Well, I suppose that settles that," said the Captain Duke, after they snuck into the library to avoid discovery.

"They're just like us," Cat giggled.

She tousled her brother's hair before Mouse swatted her away. The young boy still had an expression of concern.

"Captain, what happens when Archie leaves? Is Clara going to stay?"

The Captain Duke made to dismiss such a silly idea, but the words stuck in his throat. Of course she would stay with them. This was Clara's home now. But if they were to leave the Haven… He frowned as he considered the matter. The reasons for Clara's hurried departure the night of her engagement party were many, but protecting her brother had been one of them. After she broke things off with her fiancé, that horrid Alexander Corring fellow, she said she'd feared that he might attempt to duel her brother. One of the traitorous Robbie's revelations had been that Alex was carrying on with the pretense of their engagement to avoid his debtors. Sooner or later, Clara would need to confront him, though she seemed content to avoid the issue for now. What if her responsibility to her family outweighed her need for the crew? She was not the helpless sort. She had no need of their protection. So what reasons might compel her to stay?

Realizing that the children were now staring intently, he

brushed off their concern,

"She'll stay. Of course she'll stay. She's a pilot now."

Cat did not look convinced, though her brother seemed content to accept his response for now. The Captain left the library in search of Nessa. He needed more information on this Alexander Corring, and there was also the matter of the Haven to discuss.

The Captain Duke found Nessa in the upper gallery, poring over the latest transmission from the wireless. She had set herself to the task of figuring out Robbie's plans and tracking down his allies, channelling her fury to throw herself into the investigation with unmatched vigour.

"Ah, Captain. I've just had the latest come in from Marie—ah, Captain Buchanan."

"What is the good Captain Buchanan saying?" he asked with a smirk, sitting in a nearby chair.

Marie Buchanan—dubbed the Black Widow in the common papers after her husband's passing and the subsequent estate war—had become their greatest ally in the search for the origins of the gunpowder they had discovered on the airship they had found Clara on. Captain Buchanan was known to all and highly respected for her crew's expertise in the cross-Atlantic trade routes. It was rare for a shipment to pass without her knowledge, and she had taken it upon herself to discover what kind of plot they had become involved in. It helped, he figured, that the formidable woman had a soft spot for Nessa.

"Well, it seems that Robbie was in touch with someone at the London docks. I believe he had plans to deliver the gunpowder to its original destination—if his mutiny was successful. There are rumours of a hefty bribe."

"How did he locate the destination of the cargo? We questioned the captain of that airship after we found Clara on board. He knew nothing."

"Well, I'm not exactly sure. But I found half of a coded transmission that he failed to properly destroy in a waste bin by the wireless. I'm working on it. I think that the gunpowder might have been smuggled onto the Isle of Wight. Maybe by boat, or some other undiscoverable means. Whatever its origins, someone is bound to be missing it."

The Captain gave a wry smile. Missing it indeed. He would have preferred a version of events in which the gunpowder had not been employed to destroy half of his home.

"I've started to wonder whether Clara's presence on that ship was a coincidence," he said.

"Captain, we've already been through this. Surely you cannot believe that she had any involvement in the scheme."

"No, no, nothing like that. It's that Alexander Corring, her former fiancé. We know he has debts and we know he's desperate to avoid paying them, enough so to carry on the ruse of an engagement to Clara. An airship filled with illicit goods leaving on the same night as their engagement party… something is missing here. I want to know if he was involved in some way."

"Are you sure you're not just after a report on the man who broke Clara's heart?"

"She's hardly heartbroken," the Captain scoffed. "And

if she sees him again, I'd bet on her doing some breaking of her own thanks to your training."

Nessa laughed, "It's not that I don't agree with you. I'll look into Corring and see what I can find. And I'll see if Captain Buchanan can learn anything more about Robbie's contact in London."

"Good. There's another matter I want to discuss…"

Nessa turned and crossed her ankle over her knee, leaning back in the chair.

"Yes?"

"We need to leave the Haven."

"I know."

"I figured as much."

"I was going to give you another week to come around to it. Trick's been making progress and I didn't want to upset him any further."

"He may take it roughly, yes."

"Well, here's what I've drawn up so far," she said, pulling a stack of papers from beneath a ledger.

The Captain smiled as he looked over the rough arrangements. His crew never let him down.

"You've been planning this for some time."

"We all needed time to recover. I knew you'd see the need for it, eventually."

"Have you shown this to Clara? To Peg?"

"Of course not, Captain. I wanted to get your thoughts first."

"Yes. Yes, you're right. Nessa, I—well, thank you."

She gave him a long look, "We'll follow you anywhere, Captain."

Nessa could read his moods nearly as well as Trick could. In his dozen or so years as the Captain Duke, he had never faced a mutiny of that scale, and it shook his confidence. He sighed, and gave a nod in gratitude for her understanding.

"I'll go check in on Trick."

The Captain Duke left the room and went down the hall to find his friend. There was some larger scheme in play here, and he wanted to know more before planning their next move. He was growing tired of this game, ever trying to stay a step ahead of the Tradists and their machinations, or whoever this new player was. The landscape was changing much faster these days. This was no simple matter of raiding the Tradist ships and pushing the goods into the black market. Someone was getting greedy and it was his intention to find out who.

He rested his forehead on the doorjamb of Trick's chambers before entering. The Captain held onto a vision of a calmer life, of standing before the window of a great house with lawns stretching into the distance. In his daydream, he turned to see Clara, comfortably ensconced in an armchair by the hearth, setting down a book to smile up at him. The Captain Duke shook his head to clear it. If there was to be such a future, it was a long way off. Still, he was smiling as he entered the room.

Chapter 6: In which our heroine finds puzzles in the past

The morning light shone into the ballroom through windows that stretched to the second story. Dust motes danced through the sunbeams, illuminating the inlaid parquet flooring. Once upon a time the scuff marks had been left by dancers as the walls reverberated the sounds of revelry and life. Now, the sound of Clara's footsteps echoed back to her as she entered the room.

Clara picked a warm bun off the sideboard, buttering it as she crossed to the table to join Nessa and the children. She had just seen three of the small crews off for long-range tours, and had time to spare before the afternoon raids were sent out. Cook had taken to setting out breakfast buffet style after the destruction of the kitchens and dining hall, easier to manage with the pilot crews coming and going at different times. Cat and Mouse were already tucking into their food. Nessa's plate was untouched as she looked through a set of old logbooks. Clara sat across from her friend and poured out some of the strong coffee she had taken a liking to, ever since they acquired the beans on a raid the month before. She added a dash of milk and paused to inhale the rich aroma, sighing happily as she took the first sip. Nessa gave her a brief smile before returning to her task.

"Nessa, you really must eat," Clara admonished. "You were up before dawn this morning. The work can wait."

"The days grow shorter, it's not difficult to beat the sun."

She paused for a mouthful of egg, then continued reading as she washed it down with a sip of tea.

Cat rolled her eyes and exchanged a look with Clara before continuing her discussion with Mouse. Clara listened in on their happy chatter comparing various flight manoeuvres. The two of them clearly missed life aboard the airship. She smiled as Archie entered the hall and joined them, taking a seat beside her after filling a plate of his own.

"You know, Mouse," Clara said as he finished extolling the virtues of a dual versus single wing glider. "My brother here knows a thing or two about the mechanics behind the construction."

"Oh? Well which do you prefer?" the boy asked.

Archie looked around, "Well, I've dabbled yes. It depends on whether you seek greater stability or agility. The trick lies in how to incorporate elements of both designs into a single contraption to build upon the necessary strengths."

Mouse held a spoon halfway to his mouth, "Can you show me? Is that what you did for yours?"

"Can you build me one?" asked Cat.

"I do have some books on the theory behind their development I could lend you…"

The three of them launched into a debate on the finer mechanics of aeronautical engineering. Clara was happy to receive an education of sorts just by witnessing their enthusiasm. Her expertise lay in people, not machines, but she followed along as best she could, ignoring the deep sighs from Nessa that peppered the discussion. Finally, scrutinizing the stack of books, her curiosity could not be contained further.

"Really, Nessa. I will have the Captain ban logbooks from the table."

Nessa placed her elbows on the table, resting her chin on folded hands, "There's something bothering me about this report but I can't place my finger on it."

"Let me see," said Clara, reaching over. She studied the log while Nessa ate, turning the pages over.

"Nessa, this isn't one of ours."

"Is that not Robbie's handwriting?"

"No, but it's a similar sort of chicken scrawl. See? The dates don't match up. I swear I already transcribed ours from the summer."

"You're right," said Nessa, after examining the page in question. "The airship was nowhere near these ports. Let's go and compare."

She started to rise from the bench, but not before Clara snatched the book away again.

"First, we eat. Then I'll assist you."

Nessa considered the offer for a moment, eyeing the logbook Clara held aloft as though determining the merit in fighting her for it. The matter was resolved when, in between a sip of coffee and a mouthful of biscuit, Archie plucked the logbook from Clara's hands, with no interruption in the stream of his conversation, and sat on it.

Nessa's mouth dropped in shock, but Clara calmly returned to her meal, trading a sidelong grin with her brother over her cup. Nessa sighed and turned to her meal in earnest, and the lively conversation continued as they broke their fast.

With Archie and Mouse off to entertain themselves with glider schematics, Nessa and Clara spread out the logbooks in the study with Cat's help, matching the dates and cargos. All were bound in plain leather, made to handle the wear and tear aboard an airborne vessel. The Captain Duke was not one for embossing his books with a crest or name—Clara had begun to doubt whether the airship *had* a proper name, it currently bore the mark *Aurora's Tempest*—and they quickly determined that the extra logbook must have come from another vessel. As they traced its route and cargo, they soon realized it belonged to the airship that had carried the gunpowder.

"This is brilliant! I was certain it must have been destroyed with the ship," said Nessa.

"The final entry is the false grain shipment, the one they used as a cover for the gunpowder," pointed out Cat. "The 24th of July, the day before we found you, Clara. But they came into the tallport of the Isle of Wight on the 21st and weren't due to leave until the 28th."

Nessa frowned, "What was it that led you to choose that particular airship, Clara?"

"I'm not sure exactly, it all happened so fast. I knew they usually went straight to London so I just picked the one that looked as though it was leaving first."

"And this was after or during the party? Or when it was supposed to be happening?" asked Nessa. "I wonder why they would have left in the evening. The illicit cargo probably spooked the captain, he must have had knowledge of it then and feared discovery. Or perhaps they were trying to avoid an unexpected complication."

"Something must have happened to have them off in such a hurry. How did you discover us?" asked Clara.

"We came across that one by accident, actually. We thought we were on track to intercept a shipment of spices coming from Morocco when the ship you were on appeared. It seemed heavily laden, so we took the chance."

"How fortunate for me then. So there was no prior information on its movements? Nothing from your sources?" Clara asked.

"Not that I heard. We need more details. I need to share this with Marie. She may know some of these other shipments."

"Where is she now?" asked Clara.

"Her crew is in London. She's waiting on some Tradist summit."

"Perhaps you should pay her a visit. It's no more than a day's journey, and we can combine our resources."

"It's been some time since our paths crossed," Nessa said with a nervous laugh.

"Oh? She spoke so highly of you when we met in Whitehaven."

Nessa busied herself with tidying the logbooks, a faint blush rising on her cheeks.

"At any rate, it's a good idea. I'll ask the Captain, see

what he thinks."

Clara thought her reaction curious, but she recalled a similar attentiveness from Captain Buchanan whenever Nessa was mentioned. Her mischievous side rose up as she resolved to ensure that her friend was sent to liaise with the renowned Captain Buchanan.

Nessa pulled out a new map from the shelves that lined the room, "We'll be leaving the Haven soon. I've been working on some initial plans I'd like to hear your input on."

Clara looked over Nessa's shoulder as Cat helped to lay the map flat on the table, and scanned the list she'd drawn up.

"This could work, but we'd need to delegate by regions. If you are to be in London, we'll need to find someone for the north."

Nessa grinned, "I've been watching the crews, and checking Cat's books. I've a few pilots in mind to be regional liaisons. I'll need to pass it by the Captain and Trick, but they'll agree, I'm sure."

"With this, our central base could be anywhere as long as we keep in touch through the wireless. I've been planning to have the crews travel further afield, and this is the perfect opportunity," said Clara, chewing her bottom lip as she considered the plan. "We'll need to coordinate with Master Tims, but the scheme was developed to be decentralized. It should work…as long as we can trust the independent crews."

"Only the best and most trustworthy. And we'll have regular check-ins. I will not let Robbie's actions poison our crew further; I think this will work as a sign of our good faith. They fought for the Haven as we did. They adopted our new scheme with relish. They have more than earned our trust."

Clara nodded in agreement. The system they had developed was quite effective. They focused on targeting a series of regular ports, but had stuck to the outliers so far. They'd even had a successful run in Edinburgh. The ships' captains had come to accept these quality checks; there was hardly any resistance now. Still, they exercised caution, playing on the overstuffed bureaucracy of the Tradist association to avoid detection of their scheme. An official-looking document carried a great deal of weight, and their forgeries were now the standard by which the true papers were judged.

"Alright then. We'll have good people in place, and we'll set a meeting point for all to gather before the Hunter's Moon festivals next month. That should give us enough time."

Clara set out to coordinate the afternoon crews while Nessa and Cat plotted next week's raids. She ran her fingers over the intricate panelling as she walked through the hall, but her fingers came away grey from the fine ash that had settled into the grooves. She brushed the soot from her hands, determined to remember the Haven as it was. It was time to say goodbye to this home.

Chapter 7: In which our hero decides on a new course

The Captain Duke was walking about the grounds of the Haven with Trick, an afternoon exercise mandated by Archie to encourage his first mate's recovery. They walked in silence amidst the turning leaves, some already fallen to crunch beneath their feet. The two men stuck to the southern end of the island, the part untouched by fire. Trick's pace was slow, and the Captain matched it. His injury had impacts beyond the loss of limb. His strength was diminished by the prolonged bed rest. His balance was altered, though he had begun to compensate for it. Clara's brother had crafted a weighted armband for Trick to wear, to prevent the muscles from further atrophy. The wound still needed time to properly heal before they could move forward with a biomechanical prosthetic.

They walked until they found a fallen log that looked sturdy enough to hold them, and sat down to rest. They could see the waves of the Derwentwater lapping upon the rocky shore beyond the treeline, and the quiet rhythm filled the silence between them until Trick gave a shuddering sigh.

"Just say it, Captain."

"Say what, precisely?"

"You need to leave the Haven. We've overstayed as it is, and don't pretend it was nae for my benefit. There's too much at stake. It's time for you to leave this place behind."

The Irish always came out in his first mate when he was either extremely happy or distressed. Usually it was the former. Clearly that was not the case today. There was a heavy note in Trick's voice. He was hugging his arm close to his body in a defensive gesture, as though trying to protect himself from the world. He was not only asking the Captain to leave the Haven. He was asking to be left behind as well. The Captain stood up from the makeshift bench and turned to his friend.

"No. No, I will not hear of it. Trick Kilarney, I will have no other first mate. You've been at my side form the start. No one could replace you. Even with one good arm you're the best pilot here. The crew looks to you. I look to you." His voice cracked, "I don't know how to do this without you."

Trick stared into the trees, blinking forcefully. He was the kind of man who seemed larger than he really was by sheer force of personality. But now he sat hunched on the rotting tree, and the Captain could see the toll of age and injury. The thick, dark waves of his hair were streaked with silver at the temples. Deep lines were etched around his eyes. Still, they had only celebrated his fortieth year the summer before last, and he was by no means an old man. The wound had spread to his mind, and that was a far more difficult battle to wage. The Captain sighed and knelt before his friend.

"Trick, you will be well again. I swear it. Do not worry about the crew. Clara and Nessa have our operation well in hand, and plans, good plans, ways to expand our network beyond anything we could have dreamed a decade ago. Look at what we've built together. You saw how Keswick rallied around us in our hour of need. This is not the end.

This is not over. We will regroup and come back stronger."

Trick struggled to speak, but swallowed hard and met his eyes with a nod. The Captain put his hand on his shoulder and pulled him closer until their foreheads touched. He held his mentor until the moment passed, willing his strength to him, feeling crushed by the inexpressible emotion that threatened to overwhelm him.

They rose and brushed the dirt and soot from their clothes before making their way back towards the Haven. The Captain Duke carried the conversation with anecdotes of the crew's activities in recent weeks. His tale of Cat's new predilection for wearing an old chatelaine she'd found elicited a genuine smile, and he told of the various bits of weaponry she'd added to the keys and trinkets that hung from it.

"Little Cat is growing up too quickly, she'll want a ship of her own soon enough," said Trick.

"Cat and Mouse both, they'll never let me forget they managed the entire airship by themselves."

"Brave little ones. You're lucky they brought it back."

The Captain laughed, and earned an even broader grin from Trick. It was a small step, but an improvement nonetheless.

That evening, a table was set for an officers' dinner in the Captain Duke's study. Trick had decided to attend after all, taking his place at the Captain Duke's right hand, with Nessa seated on his left. He'd asked Clara to join them, and Archie as well. Nessa had chosen three trusted pilots to lead the regional crews: Peg, a respected and resourceful fighter;

Madge, with her cleverness and chemist's tricks; and Himmat Singh, a courageous and honourable young man. All had proven themselves in the new scheme, with sound judgement and cunning ploys.

They ate their supper and told of the days' activities. Peg had been to Keswick to meet with Master Tims and drop off a shipment of new textiles for Mrs. Cottingham. She brought news of the town's activities, now a hub for the thriving underground economy fueled by their acquisitions. They waited until their meal was finished for Nessa to bring them all up to speed on the plans to leave the Haven.

"…we'll need to sort out the assignments in the next day or so, but then the regional crews should have some flexibility in choosing their targets as long as they report their movements so that Clara can ensure the tallports are selected in good rotation," she said, looking to Clara. "They can target the ports in a cycle, regular visits appear to be well received. They'll offload their cargo in one of the four points to the black market. Master Tims has offered to set up contacts for us. And we'll continue in this fashion until the storm season, which gives us two months to find another Hav—another hideout."

"I think it best that we scatter. They'll be looking for one ship, not eleven," Clara spoke up.

The Captain Duke nodded, "It gives us more time to figure out what other forces are in play, and it will be harder to strike against us if they cannot find us. Trick? What are your thoughts?"

"Disparate groups striking in smaller factions. Robbie never knew of this, he won't be able to give us away. And any who search here will find nought but ruins. They'll think we've moved on."

The Captain Duke nodded, taking in the mood of the room, "So we are agreed then? This is the best course of action?"

There was a series of nods ands and affirmations, as each gave their consent to the plan.

"Good. Then, Peg, you'll have everything north of Derbyshire. Madge, you take the Midlands and Wales. Himmat, you'll have the southwest. Nessa, you said you'd traced your leads to London?"

"Yes, and then the threads are lost. I think it best if I liaise with Captain Buchanan and her crew. If we combine our resources, we may be able to discover the source of the gunpowder. She has far greater reach than I."

"Good. I will accompany you. I feel our London 'friend' may be needed. His connections could be of use to us. We'll cover the southeast."

"Captain Duke, if I may, I have a home close to the campus in Reading," piped in Archie "It would be ideal if we were to continue Trick's treatment without significant interruption. And I'll have greater access to the tools and resources needed for his recovery. I believe Professor Sewell would welcome the idea. If you wish, of course, Mr. Kilarney."

Trick nodded, "It's a kind invitation, Archie, and I thank ye for it. If it's no imposition…"

"Not at all! I've a large house on Kendrick Road, a stone's throw from Lovelace. Far too much for a bachelor scholar such as myself. The staff will be pleased to have someone to appreciate their efforts."

"Then perhaps you won't mind greater company," said

the Captain Duke. "Trick, Clara will accompany you. Cat and Mouse too. They'll be able to run the scheme from there, and a respectable family visit is the perfect cover for our enterprise. It will raise fewer questions than sending you alone."

Archie's mouth gaped, and he turned to Clara. There was a strange look in her eyes, but it faded to a stony expression. Lifting her chin, she met the Captain's gaze.

"If that's what you think best."

"In that case," began Archie, with an appropriate degree of caution. "I would be pleased to welcome all of you into my home."

The Captain Duke could feel Clara's displeasure as a palpable thing. Surely she must understand. It was the perfect solution. Trick would not feel abandoned, and she and the children would be safe to pursue their work in her brother's home.

"Good, if that is settled, there's one more matter to be addressed. Clara, I have spoken with the crew and all are in agreement. I name you our new Quartermaster."

He raised a glass, and all followed. Clara wore an expression of surprise, but reached for her glass and raised it with a tight smile.

"I accept."

They drank deeply, and more toasts followed; to the Haven, to the new regional officers, to Trick's recovery. But there was a melancholy that weighed on their attempts at merriment. Even when their group joined the pilots in the hall to announce their impending departure. They opened every keg they had 'liberated' in recent months and would not be taking with them. The ballroom rang with raucous laughter as the crews received their appointments and said farewell to friends they might not see until the Harvest Moon.

The Captain Duke left the festivities before the drink could get to him. He wanted a clear head for what was to come. He roamed the halls, crossing the span of neglected corridors until he came to the ruins. A full moon cast the ashy remains in an eerie light, where shadows tugged at furtive memories and intrinsic fears. The island was tranquil, and the night was dark. Over the sounds of the party behind him, he could just make out the faint lapping of waves. And then… steps. They sounded faint behind him as they drew near. He did not move, but she took up the space beside him in the doorframe.

"A Quartermaster," said Clara. "You honour me."

She did not make it sound like a distinction of great respect.

"You earned it. The crew holds you in reverence."

"The crew."

"Yes, of course. Do you doubt them?"

"Them? No."

He risked a glance in her direction. Her face was a mask of stone.

"What?" she demanded, still looking out to the jagged silhouette of the charred forest.

"I thought you'd be happier."

"I'm happy."

“That… does not sound happy.”

He watched as her chest rose and fell in a great sigh before she turned to meet his eyes.

“I’m pleased you find value in my little stratagems.” She paused, then made to leave, “Excuse me, I have a great deal of packing to do if we are to move our operations tomorrow.”

The Captain Duke reached out to place a hand on her arm.

“Clara— “

“Yes?”

His words failed him. He searched for something to set things right between them. A means of expressing how much she had come to mean to him, why it was so critical that she go to Reading, safe and sound and far from any who would wish revenge upon her. He cupped her face in his hands and tried to memorize the curve of her cheek and the way her lashes framed her eyes. But what right did he have to prolong this farewell? Instead, he dropped his hands, and stepped back. There was an unmet challenge in her gaze as she curtsied and turned into the Haven.

“Good bye, Captain.”

Too many good byes for a too uncertain future. They knew, all of them, that the end of their easygoing days had come and gone, long before they had realized. The Captain Duke leaned his head back against the frame and slid down to rest on the threshold.

Chapter 8: In which our heroine finds a genius solution

Clara paced back and forth across the deck of the airship. She'd been restless all day; the further they flew from the Haven, the more agitated she became. Not even the sensation of gliding through the clean, sharp air could still her nerves, and the day was cloudy so there was no sunshine to cheer her. She was tempted to engage in busywork, rechecking the lines and altitude or such, but she did not wish to cause offence with Mouse at the wheel. Besides, Archie was glued to the young pilot's side, and if he noticed her state of bother he would want to discuss it. Both Cat and Trick were sulking in their own way – Cat taking up residence in the lookout, Trick declaring exhaustion and retreating to the cabin.

Clara went to the rail of the foredeck and tried to calm herself with deep breaths. Her mind was racing, but she was not yet ready to dig deeper into the source of her irritation. She picked at the paint until she could see the light ash of the airship's hull beneath. It was a slower model with bulky airbags and propellers that steered its lazy journey through the skies, painted a cheerful shade of blue with bright purple trim.

When they'd found that they needed to expand their fleet in order to carry out their scheme, they had canvassed the local dealers first. *Flutterby Hum* had been a bonus to the other seven ships they had selected, a gift that their contact had insisted they accept as a token of his favour. Clara suspected the aircraft had been sitting in the lot for some time. It was rather…bold, and not at all suited to their desire to be as bland and un-noteworthy as possible. Still, it was a solid little ship, quite steady with comfortable furnishings below. And so, the Captain had taken it on and repurposed it as a shuttle. A surplus ship, but one that would not be out of place in a town such as Reading.

Clara frowned and flicked a chip of paint into the aether. The River Thames wound its way through the landscape below, guiding their path. She let out her breath in a huff and turned away from the view. Archie and Mouse were staring. She gave a smile and small wave to the two at the helm, and after a glance up at Cat, decided she'd rather risk Trick's ire than stay on deck.

The plush furnishings had somewhat survived the previous owner's attempt to repurpose the craft as a common aircab. There were large windows lining the main galley at the aft of the ship, complete with overstuffed armchairs bolted to the floor and an area set up to hold a tea service. Trick was sitting in a great blue wingback that faced the stern, looking back to his former home as he clutched his arm. Clara curled up on a nearby settee of a shocking orange hue, and the two of them sat in silence for a long while. They watched as the trees turned to field, then forest again, divided by the river and its tributaries.

"Trick?" she asked finally.

He acknowledged her with a slow nod.

"I wish we had the crew with us. I know it was my plan, but I don't like this—all of us split up like this."

He turned his face to her, and Clara could see the pain

shadowing his eyes. Heart shattered, she came to kneel by his side, taking his good hand.

"Pay me no mind, I worry about such silly things. And now I've gone and upset you."

He shook his head, "No, not at all. Don't fret—it helps to keep my mind from darker thoughts."

"Then mine will be of little help. I just—I think I worry that I could wake up tomorrow and have it all be a dream. Even on the raids, it still felt as though we had our own little world. I fear we may never have that again."

"You will always be a child of two worlds. You and the Captain have that in common. But he'll not be giving up his crew. He'll bring us all back together ere long. Besides, he has a soft spot for ye, aye?"

A half smile, but a real one. Clara felt a blush growing on her cheeks.

"Perhaps, but—," she started, before realizing she did not yet have the words.

"But you thought he'd want you by his side."

She struggled to express herself as she felt the flush rising on her cheeks, "I wanted to be asked. It's not that I didn't want to accompany you, or spend more time with my brother, it's just…"

Trick sighed, "You've the soul of an adventurer, Miss Clara. I've seen it since the first time ye saved our skins. But you're a woman of action, and the Captain is a thinker. It's how we've managed to stay ahead of the Tradists all this time. They never expected someone as clever as the Captain Duke to get in their way. And between the two of ye, we'll know soon what kind of scheme they're cooking. They're well outmatched."

"So we figure out their plan and stop them." She shook her head, "Then what?"

"You want a fortune teller? I know of a decent one near Galway."

Clara narrowed her eyes, but Trick gave a bitter laugh.

"The future holds no certainty at all, Miss Clara. I know that better than most," he said, gesturing with the stump of his arm. The humour faded, the pain returned. "The measure of a person is in how they face their circumstances, or change them, like you did."

"Like you will," she replied.

Trick took a deep breath, "I will see Archie's professor, but I make no promises. I'm not a young man any more. I'm willing to accept my fate."

"But you told the Captain—,"

"I told the Captain what he needed to hear so he could do his duty by the crew. I will not be a burden."

"You are no burden at all," she protested. "Trick, we need you. We rely on your counsel. You speak of the Captain's cleverness, but you say nothing of your own. He would not have come this far without you, none of us would. Nessa may well have dropped me at the nearest hamlet had it not been for you."

"Aye. Which is why I know the Captain will be back. He'll need you now, Clara."

"I—pardon?"

"You inspire him to be a better man. And you, in the short time I've known you, you've gone from a headstrong debutante to a respected leader among the crew. But the both of ye need to finish growing before you can know where your story leads."

Clara mulled over Trick's words. Below, shadows moved in great sweeps over the countryside from the clouds that dotted the sky. The sun had painted a silhouette of the airship too, steadily tacking their progress over forest and field. Villages started to dot the landscape, growing closer together as they neared their destination. It was a tranquil scene, but for Clara it felt like the calm before the storm. She took a deep breath, her mind no clearer than before, but tranquil at last. When it came time for her to return above deck to assist with the landing, she squeezed Trick's hand, wishing some of her strength into her friend.

"There will be a future for us—all of us—and you will be a part of it," she said.

The words came out with an unexpected intensity, surprising both of them. But Clara swallowed the lump in her throat and waited for Trick to nod in affirmation before going above.

Reading was an interesting cluster of shops and houses—larger than Clara had expected, but still carrying a sense of quaint charm amidst the more obvious signs of its position at the forefront of the recent wave of invention. There were turbine generators on all the houses, and some of the public buildings even bore clusters of the photovoltaic cells which had become the latest darling of the scientific community. There was a quadruple tallport by the docks, but one of more recent design stretched above the new university. Three matching tiers stretched out to them in welcome.

"Oh you needn't bother with the ropes," Archie called, as she began to prepare for the docking.

"What do you mean?" she asked.

"The Professor is expecting us. We're going to test our new gangplank."

Clara looked at Cat, who had climbed down from her perch, and shrugged. They stood together at the rail to watch as Mouse steered them toward the highest tier, following her brother's instructions. A lone figure stood at the end of one of the spokes. Around half of the ports were taken up by all manner of vessels, a mix of the sleek and elegant Skyflyer-class hybrids with older, wooden vessels. There was one of such bright trappings and ornate design that it must have come all the way from India. The new campus must draw students from across the empire, Clara thought, as a flash of light caught her eye. A sunbeam had broken through the clouds to illuminate the tallport and the young woman who stood before them, skirts tied back to drape neatly around a bright, mechanical leg.

Their attention was quickly stolen by the strange trappings of the port. As Archie manoeuvred the airship into position, the Professor pulled a lever and a metallic gangplank unfurled toward them, piece by piece, until it had latched onto the hull, stabilizing the airship before expanding into a small stairway. It was an odd sight, and struck a chord of discomfort in Clara. She regarded it with apprehension, but after checking the fastenings she took a breath and stepped onto the solid platform. By all rights, it should have been Trick greeting their new host as the highest ranking officer. But for the moment it was Clara's responsibility, and she held her head high as she walked down the gangway.

"Welcome to Lovelace University, Lady Whittington," said the woman, reaching out a hand in assistance.

"Please, call me Clara. And you must be the professor my brother has told me so much about," she replied.

Archie cleared his throat loudly from the platform behind her, and she stepped aside to make room for him.

"Professor," he said, with a slight bow and a smile before turning to their party. "May I introduce you to Professor Georgina Jameson Sewell, the finest scholar of biomechanical apparatus and manipulations."

She was younger than Clara had expected. Her raven black hair was pulled back into a twist, and a pair of magnifying spectacles rested on top of her head.

"The original scholar, if I've heard correctly. My brother raves about your genius," Clara said, amused by the faint blush that crossed both of their cheeks. "I am ever so grateful for your offer to help our friend."

"A friend of the Whittingtons is a friend of mine. I will certainly do everything in my power to ensure he receives the best treatment."

Introductions were made as the others crossed over. Trick came next, a heavy coat draped over his shoulders to hide his injury, and he cradled his arm close to his body. Mouse stayed by his side, with a look of concern, but he gave the first officer his space. Cat followed behind, shoulders thrown back as she took in the professor and the campus below.

"Professor, this is our dear friend, Trick Kilarney, and his niece and nephew, Catherine and Morris. They'll be joining us for the duration of his treatment."

"Come, come. We'll send the porter for your things," said Professor Sewell. "You must join me for tea before you continue home. Mr. Kilarney, I'm particularly interested in learning more of your situation."

Trick mumbled something in response, but it came out as more of a grunt. The weathered pirate was looking distinctly ill at ease. Clara stepped in to thank their host and accept the Professor's invitation. Then their little band made their way down the elevator and towards a grand building at the end of a manicured path.

Clara stayed by Trick's side as they walked, hoping that his mood would improve as he became more familiar with his surroundings. She took in the gardens and the students strolling between the buildings. A small group was playing with some number of small, complex gadgets as they sat on the grass. She smiled at the camaraderie on display as they tested their inventions against one another. But her notice was drawn to Professor Sewell and her brother, walking before them. Her gait was brisk and natural, no obvious signs of impact from the mechanical nature of her limb. They could see the delicate gears as they worked to create the fluid movement. She stole a quick glance at Trick to see if he was watching too, but his eyes were fixed on the ground before him.

"The modifications to the upper level gangplank worked beautifully. You've improved on my designs," said Archie, keeping up the flow of conversation.

"For the most part, but just last week the docking system on the second tier took a chip out of Lady Palmer's favourite coach. The interns did their best but I would be in your debt if you would review their work."

"Of course, Professor," he answered, and Clara could hear the smile in his voice as they entered the building.

They settled into an elegant drawing room as the college's staff set out a tea service laden with biscuits. They were still in their travel clothes, Clara realized, but the Professor did not seem to mind. She herself had the appearance of one for whom clothing was an afterthought, giving little care for propriety or the expectations of her gender in favour of more pressing concerns. Clara approved. She had almost forgotten the habit in polite society of changing one's clothes thrice or more in a day, a ritual she did not miss.

"Please, take a biscuit. We have an abundance of them," said Professor Sewell with a gentle smile, offering the children a plate of the treats. Cat and Mouse were sitting ramrod straight, feet tucked beneath the chairs, hands folded in their laps. But at her offer, Mouse relaxed a little, taking one from the plate before passing it to his sister.

"You know, I actually missed these," said Archie, taking three and stuffing one in his mouth, whole. Clara smirked. Swallowing, he licked his lips and wiped his mouth with a napkin. "Huntley and Palmers, the town is quite famous for them."

"Oh, like the tins?" asked Cat, her interest peaked.

Professor Sewell brightened, "Yes! We have a collection of them on display in the Founder's Hall. Mrs. Eddie Poulton—formerly Miss Emily Palmer—was a student here. One of my classmates, actually. Her family donated the land for the campus. I'd be more than happy to have one of my assistants give you a tour once you've settled in."

"Thank you, I would like that."

"Excellent!"

The Professor was beaming, but the smile and manners did not quite suit her. She did not seem false, only very eager to make a good impression. Clara looked around the room, taking in the varying degrees of discomfort. Cat was warming to their host, but her guard was up. She was being ever so polite and distant, far from her usual self. Mouse bore a guilty look as he tried to sip his tea but ended up slurping it noisily. He kept glancing at the nearby shelves and Clara knew he was resisting the urge to inspect all the artefacts and knickknacks on display. Trick was too quiet, too reserved, and rather out of his element. She wondered if they had made a mistake taking him from the Haven and the impact it might have on his recovery. She was glad, in the end, that the Captain had sent her and the children to stay by Trick's side. It looked as though he would need them. Only Archie seemed oblivious to the tension in the room, munching on biscuits without a care, and teasing his supervisor in a rather unprofessional manner. However, as Clara watched, she saw Professor Sewell begin to relax, even daring to make a few jests as they caught up on the events of the previous weeks. Clara hid a smile behind her teacup as she realised her brother's leisurely affectations were his way of helping her to feel more comfortable.

"And then Jenny—bless her soul—she mixed up the hydraulics and sent Davis tumbling backwards as soon as he tried to take a step. Honestly, that girl is a genius wrencher but she cannot tell her left from her right. I've sent her back to practicing on the autobaubles."

"I have an idea," Archie replied. "I met a charming

gentleman inventor on my trip—Master Tims, he runs the general store in Keswick—and he had the most ingenious solution while teaching his young daughter to assist him. He tied a red ribbon around one of her wrists—red for her right hand. I think Jenny might excel with a bit of accommodation in her training."

"What a charming solution, how old is the girl?"

"I can't be sure. Clara, do you know?"

"Lottie Tims? No more than four, I'd say."

"Lottie will be four in the spring. She's quite a smart 'un though," offered Cat.

"And already getting into mechanical manipulations, just darling! I should very much like to meet her, perhaps she will study here one day. It's wonderful to see them start so young," said Professor Sewell.

"You were one of the first students here, if Archie's told me correctly," Clara smiled.

"I had to beg for it, but Mrs. Somerville allowed me to join the first class. There were only six of us at the time, and I was barely 12 years old. But I had been in regular correspondence with her since I was eight, so it didn't take much convincing. All of the first classes were young women she had mentored in some capacity, or their daughters. Ada Lovelace was once a pupil of hers, you know? It's how the Lovelace family was compelled to give such a generous donation to the school."

It was Clara's interest that peaked now, "I've heard stories of her work with Charles Babbage."

"We have a collection of her papers in the library. The

Department of Analytics is still in its early stages, but we have an arrangement between Lovelace and Oxford to share our resources in the advancement of its work. Similar to the arrangement with Archie's department, though he was the first visiting scholar to come our way."

"How do you mean?" Clara asked, intrigued by the colour rising in her brother's cheeks.

"Well, usually our students complete their studies here, and seek further education at Oxford, Cambridge or abroad. When we first received his request we were not quite sure how to proceed."

"What she means is they doubted my scholarly intentions," he said, laughing at her protestations. "Now, now, Professor. I know I caused a bit of a disruption. Let's just say that it became clear through my studies that I would forever be playing catch-up unless I could receive tutelage from the best in the world. And all of the papers on the subject were authored by a G. J. Sewell."

"He started sending me letters, you see. My published papers are always some months behind our current innovations. We're able to adapt the technology much faster than in the initial stages of development."

"And then you did the lecture in London that I attended."

"You thought I was my own wife!"

"And you quickly disabused me of such a horrid notion. I spent the next six months apologizing."

"He did no such thing. But he did send along an original Arabic text on algebraic calculations that was of particular value in developing a new theorem on the hydraulic systems."

"Well, would you have ever spoken to me again—let alone accepted my application as a visiting scholar—if I'd sent flowers?"

Clara felt a small kick on her chair from Trick, and quickly closed her gaping mouth, covering her amusement by seeking out another biscuit.

The Professor flushed as she recalled their company.

"Of course, you must all be tired from your travels. Do take the rest of the day to settle in. I have some work to finish, but I hope you will join me for dinner this evening."

Clara accepted the invitation and their little group boarded a small mechanicab to take them around the corner to Archie's home, a respectable house on Kendrick Road. The household staff collected their belongings and showed them to their rooms. The children were bemused by the offers of assistance to set out their clothes for the evening. Thankfully, they each had a set of fine clothing, courtesy of Mrs. Cottingham, rarely used and usually worn as part of some scheme. It would serve their needs just fine.

Clara settled in for an afternoon nap, vowing to quiz her brother on his friendship with the Professor that evening. If she could not act on her intentions towards the Captain Duke, she could at least meddle a little in her brother's life. She would make sure her brother did not make the same mistake she did, leaving important things unsaid. She closed her eyes and dreamed of blue eyes framed by tangled red locks.

Chapter 9: In which our hero meets an ally in the sky

Their departure had been uneventful. Before, the Captain Duke had always been eager to leave the Haven in search of adventure with nary a glance behind. This time, he had stood with Nessa at the stern as they watched their home disappear into the trees, half-destroyed, blackened by smoke and streaked by rain. The grand old manor bore its wounds with dignity, but the Captain was struck by the frailty of it all. More, he was stunned by his own need for the Haven to be solid, secure. As a man who lived most of his life in the skies, he had thought himself immune to the pull of permanence. In truth, he needed that anchor, and was wondering if his adventures had been made possible in part because he always had it to return to.

It had been harder to part with Trick. It was not that they never were apart; Trick usually spent the storm season visiting his father, while the Captain had his own pursuits. It was the uncertainty of whether he would ever again have the privilege of flying with his first mate by his side. Though Trick had regained a measure of his former joviality, there was a weariness to his manner. His smile did not always reach his eyes. It was good that Clara would be with him to ensure his recovery progressed.

But the hardest goodbye had been to the children. Cat had taken on a stoicism at odds with her usual cheerfulness. It was while they saw Madge's crew off that she'd cornered him, out of earshot of her brother.

"You swore you would never leave us behind."

Her look of betrayal cut him to his core.

"I would never. You'll be with Trick still, and Clara."

"But we want to fly, Captain. We want to come with you and Nessa."

"You are needed in Reading, Cat. I cannot leave Trick unprotected in his current state and you'll be busy assisting Clara in organizing the crews. You and your brother will hardly notice the time passing."

"I will not be tucked away like a child anymore. It's not fair," she scowled.

The Captain Duke had crossed his arms,

"You asked for greater responsibility and I am giving it to you. Protect Trick and watch over your brother. Assist Clara. Those are your orders, pilot."

He didn't think it kind to mention that her brother certainly felt differently about the matter. He'd hardly left Archie's side since his arrival at the Haven, and had taken to tinkering with the designs from the books loaned to him. In truth, he thought it good for the boy to see more of the world beyond the deck of an airship. The Captain had always felt it his duty to protect them, to try to preserve something of the childhood that was stolen from them with the death of their father. Cat rarely spoke of how she and her brother had made their way to find his crew, but he knew that she had seen hardship that no child should have to endure. It was not his place to coddle her. And so, he fought his initial impulse to ruffle her curls and send her off.

Instead, he placed a steady hand on her shoulder,

"Cat, growing up does not mean getting to do as you like. We are all bound by our duty to one another. Some days those duties weigh heavier than most. You have proven yourself to be a capable pilot, but I must request this of you. I know they'll be safe in your hands."

Now the Captain Duke leaned against the rail, looking over the landscape below, wishing he was better at taking his own advice. He could feel the morning air fresh on his face as he breathed in the sky. This was where he was happiest, high above the earth. And yet, he was unsettled. He felt at odds with the world. He wanted someone to act against, no more of these nebulous plots and schemes. Deep in thought, he hardly noticed the disturbance in his crew until Nessa tugged at his arm.

"Captain? We have visitors."

"How—?"

Then, he saw the gliders. Three of them flew down as though originating from the clouds themselves. It must have been a massive airship to reach such heights. The pilots looped through the air, banking against the winds, aiming for his ship. His small crew readied themselves for a fight, but Nessa held them back with a laugh and the Captain soon recognized their guests as well.

The first of the pilots landed with an elegant flip as she collapsed the wings. Her companions were more subdued, but just as graceful. As the leader removed her goggles, the Captain Duke walked forward.

"Captain Buchanan, an unexpected surprise."

She reached out to shake his hand, "I hope you don't

mind our joining you a little early. The skies of London have been rife with upjumped sergeants and I thought you might appreciate some backup."

Nessa came to stand at his elbow. The air between the two women seemed to hum despite their formality. The distinguished captain stood as tall as Nessa, hair drawn back in tidy locs to cascade down her back. Her cream jacket was tailored to suit her figure and complemented her dark complexion.

"It pleases me to see you looking well, Nessa."

"It has been far too long, Marie."

Captain Buchanan extended a hand, and Nessa raised it to her lips for a kiss. Her breath caught as their eyes met… then, with a shake of her head and a laugh, she pulled Nessa into her arms and kissed her.

When they broke apart, Nessa looked flustered but happy. And Marie Buchanan—the captain who conquered the Atlantic trade routes, the Black Widow who won over the Empire with her fearless resolve—was positively glowing.

"I've been waiting some time to do that and I'll not wait a second more."

The two seemed happy to continue in their own world, and the Captain was loathe to interrupt such a reunion but the crew was rather distracted. He cleared his throat to remind them of their duties, and they quickly returned to their work.

"Your concern for our welfare is touching," he said. "I'm quite certain your presence is appreciated."

"Anything for a friend," she smiled, looking at Nessa. Then she grew serious. "Alice here has been assisting with the mystery of the stolen gunpowder and knows as much as any of us. And I've brought along my bosun, he knows the city well and has a number of useful connections. Both will help with anything you need during your time here."

"And how much longer will you be in the city?" he asked.

"It is uncertain, but the negotiations with the Tradists have hit a standstill, shall we say, and the storm season is fully underway in the Caribbean. It will be another month at this rate."

"I am sorry to hear that. If there's anything we can do to help, you have only to ask."

"Good. I may have a favour to call on—but that is a discussion best saved for later."

They continued their discussion in his quarters, maps and books spread across the large table. But, with no new information, the conversation quickly devolved into catching up on the latest manoeuverings of the Tradists, the political climate of London and news from Captain Buchanan's extensive network of pilots. Her company was now based in Saint Vincent, a volcanic island at the border of the Atlantic and Caribbean Sea, but her airships travelled to every corner of the empire and beyond. They traded goods, mostly, but she had long held that information was also valuable currency.

The rest of the trip to London was uneventful, particularly as Captain Buchanan's *Fregata* tracked their progress from above the clouds. The air was filled with airships of every shape and size, making the Captain Duke's galleon seem quaint and unremarkable by comparison. It had been months, but the weft and sway of the urban hubbub was comforting in its own way. And so the Captain privately celebrated his homecoming, a secret known to but a handful of souls.

Chapter 10: In which our heroine is the cause of offence and inspiration

Their days fell into a charming routine. Clara would spend the mornings sending out new assignments over the wireless, tracking the Tradist ships and going over the port logs to select their next targets. Cat would take care of the maps and logbooks, charting out the most secure paths and ensuring that safe havens were close by. Each of the crews would report their positions throughout the day, giving the names of the captains they had encountered and updates on the conditions of the port towns. Master Tims' black market connections had proven invaluable. There was a growing discontent among the towns with the monopoly exercised by the Tradists and their sympathizers. The prices for many common goods were out of reach for many, and poorer families were struggling to feed and clothe themselves.

Lunch was set out by the household staff, and Archie would often join them if his research permitted. Mouse was always at his ankles, but her brother did not seem to mind. In fact, he told Clara privately, Mouse was a better assistant than the grad student Oxford had sent for him, and the Lovelace students had adopted the orphaned boy as a sort of mascot. He told them all of how Mouse had solved a complicated equation by himself while their team was still discussing how to proceed. His logic was sound, but with no formal training he had no way to teach the others how to solve it. And so Archie had taken it upon himself to learn as much from Mouse as he did from Lovelace.

In the afternoons, they walked over to the campus together. Clara spent her time in Lovelace's extensive libraries, examining their primary sources on the trade laws enacted after the formal dissolution of the East India Company in 1874. The main library was a grand, imposing affair, with marble columns and three stories of bookshelves, linked by balconies that soared overhead. But the Southern Reading Room was Clara's favourite. It was tucked away in the third floor solarium with a view of the city spread out into the distance.

She could see the airships travelling to and fro, imagining herself on them once again. It had been over a month since she'd been able to practice her gliding. Their extended stay at the Haven had put her training on hold. But she did not suffer the loss so greatly as Cat. She knew the girl ached to be in the skies again, although she was doing her best to be patient, likely for Trick's sake. And, well, he needed all their patience.

Since their arrival, he had done the bare minimum necessary to improve his condition. His exercises were performed dutifully, morning and night. He submitted to the poking and prodding of the physicians. He answered Professor Sewell's questions and allowed her to take his measurements. He ate the food that was put before him. He complained of nothing. And yet, it was apparent to all that he was going through the motions of life without actually living. When left to his own devices, Clara would catch him staring into the middle distance, his face bare of any emotion.

For the frequency of her visits to the Kendrick Road house, Archie had given up a small study to Professor Sewell as a workroom, to allow her better access to her equipment. Her mechanical leg was more than up to walking the distance, but it would have been taxing and taken valuable time away from her research. Even still, her team of protégés would be summoned to run back and forth for her, fetching the various tools and materials she required for her work.

Clara was impressed by the Professor's devotion to their friend. At first she had suspected it to be on her brother's behalf. But as she grew to know Professor Sewell, she realised her driving force ran far deeper. Her endless patience and optimism, the careful way she treated Trick's arm as an injury and not a disfigurement. In spite of his melancholy—perhaps because of it—she kept up a stream of cheerful encouragement, taking the smallest improvement as an achievement of merit. And Archie, always, was at her side to support and reassure, his genuine joy in her abilities spilling over into effusive praise at every opportunity. It was rare for them to spend an evening apart, with invitations flowing in both directions for dinners with the university faculty or private suppers with their new little crew.

It was one such evening that found all of them seated in the parlour of Archie's home, laughing over a tale of Clara's training to be a proper young lady.

"Poor Mrs. Ellington, she tried to have her play the flute every afternoon. And every day I'd listen to the fruitless whistles, until one day Clara managed the most piercing shriek. And the shrieking whistles continued for all of three days before Father decided that was the end of the music lessons."

"I thought I was rather getting the hang of it at the end," Clara laughed. "But I'm happy to leave it to the true virtuosos, like Trick."

A brief smile crossed his face, before fading into a mask of such pain that it tore at Clara's heart.

"Trick, I'm sorry. Please, don't get up. I only meant—I didn't mean—"

He gripped his shoulder, collapsing into himself, chest heaving for air as he struggled for composure. Cat rose to go to him, but he waved her off. He would not meet their eyes, but—with a great swallow and a deep, shaking breath—he did his best to assuage their concern.

"I know ye meant nothing by it. But all the same, I think I'll retire early tonight."

"Trick, please stay. It's not as though you'll never play again," responded Professor Sewell, with a look of genuine confusion. "You're nearly ready for a prosthetic, you'll be able to do just as much as before and likely more."

After a heavy pause, Trick replied in barely more than a whisper.

"It will not be the same."

"Of course it won't, it will be better! This new arm will be unbreakable. Just imagine what you'll be able to do. It will have ten times the strength of the average man."

"You cannot know—," he started, before glancing at the golden leg framed by the layered ruffles of her skirts.

Professor Sewell narrowed her eyes, "I cannot know what, exactly?"

He stood, clutching his shoulder, "I've accepted my lot. I wish you would all do the same. It is no favour to keep hold of such false hopes, and worse to pretend they have some chance at reality."

"But Trick, you've seen Professor Sewell's work. If there's any chance…" said Clara.

"Can she give me back the feeling of drawing my bow across the strings? Can she stop the phantom pains that plague my mind? Can she give me back my dignity?"

Trick was shouting now, shocking Clara and all the room into a laden silence as he continued.

"No. She cannot. I am a cripple, just as she is. And no matter your playacting, there's no magic in this world that will give me my arm back."

Professor Sewell was immediately on her feet, but she addressed Trick's back as he made his way to the door.

"I am no cripple."

Bursting into tears, she fled through the opposite door, leaving the assembled company to gape at each other. Cat, as usual, was the first to collect herself.

"We'll take Trick," she said, gesturing to her brother. "You two go find the Professor."

Professor Sewell stormed into her makeshift workroom, skirts swishing around her mechanical leg. Clara and Archie followed behind, at a distance of reasonable caution with respect to the esteemed inventor's state of agitation. Peeking around the doorframe, Clara watched as she turned about the room, stuffing papers and drawings into a large brown satchel. Archie pushed past her to enter the den of the lioness, hands raised in supplication.

"Professor, please, he did not mean what he said."

He was ignored.

"Professor?"

The woman continued to whirl about the room, gathering her belongings. Charts and quills and tools of measurement, all were thrown together in a jumbled mess. The brass mechanisms of her clockwork limb flashed in the light of the gas lamps. Clara could see the cogs and gears working in perfect, sublime synchronicity as the Professor circled Archie as though he were invisible. Then, he reached out to pluck the sheath of papers from her hand, forcing her to pause.

"Georgie."

For a half-second, Clara thought her brother was about to be pummeled. Instead, the Professor's face crumpled and she collapsed into his arms with a sob. At his look of complete shock, Clara believed her brother might have preferred a blow. She mimed for him to comfort the crying woman and he awkwardly patted her head. Throwing her hands up in the air, Clara leaned against the doorjamb to watch the tableau before her. Archie rolled his eyes and half-turned away from her, smoothing the Professor's hair and murmuring something inaudible as he held her close. After a moment, Professor Sewell pulled away, sniffing and attempting to blot her eyes with a handkerchief.

"Please, excuse me, I—I never—," she began, "I hate that word. Cripple. I am no cripple. And how dare he—Oh!" Professor Sewell stomped her golden foot and crossed the room to sit in a high-backed chair.

Archie gestured at Clara to assist him in operating the tea-making device, and within minutes the three of them were seated in the midst of the now-messy workspace drinking a steep brew as they waited for the Professor to collect herself. Archie prepared the tea for Georgina—no sugar, a dash of milk—and within a few sips, the distraught woman had visibly relaxed.

"Thank you, Archie. I do hate to lose my temper."

"And I do hate to see you so distressed."

"When I was young—," Professor Sewell started, setting her tea aside. "I loved to dance. My family had a large home in the country and all our neighbours would come to our little soirees. I always begged my father to permit me to stay up past my bedtime and he would graciously oblige—but only for three more dances. The musicians would humour me, drawing out the last song as long as they could, and then I would bid one and all good night. That was before the accident.

"I don't remember much of it. Rather, I remember the afterwards more than the incident itself. My father was crying; he had tears on his cheeks when I woke up. But he was crying because he was happy, he said. Happy that I was alive.

"I had a chair at first, but I was a restless child and crutches could only take me so far. In their efforts to distract me, they brought me books. Books on every subject you can imagine. The ballroom was converted into a library that stretched to the second storey of our home. And when my reading material was insufficient, they encouraged my correspondence with the authors.

"One of my early champions was Mrs. Somerville, as you know, who indulged my queries and pushed me to pursue my studies. She helped my parents secure the best tutors, and they, in turn, humoured my early inventions. It started as a means for my own independence. I hated having to ask for assistance when looking through our library. So, I learned the principles of mechanical design and made up a conveyance that could reach every single shelf. It was rather primitive, of course; I had the household staff work for weeks to install tracks and a pulley system that could bear my weight. Then I used what I had learned from the writings of Babbage and Lovelace to program my device. I could sit in a sling and enter the desired coordinates, and my invention would convey me to any part of the room I so desired.

"My father hated the thing; he worried that I would fall. But my mother understood why I wanted it, why I needed it so badly, and supervised a number of improvements herself. And I learned there was no such thing as barriers, only possibilities that had not yet been realized. So I set about reshaping the world to suit my needs."

The Professor paused to sip her tea, "I suppose that is why I react so strongly to being labelled by such terms. They have never defined my reality, nor the reality I have worked all my life to help others achieve."

Clara spoke up, "I never knew the story behind your inventions. But, I understand now."

"Georgie?" Archie asked, leaning forward.

"Yes?"

"When the accident happened, you were very young. Trick, however, has not had the benefit of time to adjust to his new circumstances, nor the advantage of your outlook."

Professor Sewell sighed, "I suppose you are correct."

"So, perhaps it might be necessary to treat the symptoms before the cause. We must lift his mood if we are to convince him to embrace your methods."

"Well, for me it was the library," she said, after considering his words. "But for Trick?"

"Music," Clara offered.

"Music… Music! His violin! Oh! Archie, my notes!" Professor Sewell shoved her tea aside and ran to the large desk at the centre of the room, pulling a quill from the half-packed satchel and dipping it in an old inkwell, blotting on a soiled handkerchief while Archie scrambled to assist. Clara was stunned by the flurry of it all. The two worked in concert, as Archie seemed to have an inhuman prescience for what Professor Sewell required.

Clara smiled and slowly backed out of the room to leave the two geniuses to their work, lost to a world of their own invention.

Chapter 11: In which our hero receives uncommonly good advice

The Captain Duke ducked into a doorway as his quarry cast a suspicious glance over his shoulder. The streets of London were filled with people rushing home for the evening meal. The sun, obscured by omnipresent clouds, was setting earlier and earlier as autumn took hold and the city was now cast in desaturated tones of grey. A cool wind sent dead leaves swirling around his feet. He had traded his long blue coat for a slate jacket that blended into the crowds and his bright hair was tucked beneath a respectable black hat. He did his best to escape notice as the man he was following paused to look over his shoulder once more before continuing down an alleyway.

The Captain proceeded to stroll at a regular pace down the street. He entered a glove shop across the way as he spied on the alley, positioning himself to see down its length as the shop girl made her pitch. A few well-placed questions and the young woman was off to the back of the store to fetch more samples as he browsed the wares at the front window. The man had disappeared. There was an unmarked door about halfway down, with no handle on the outside. Deciding it best not to prod the situation further than necessary, he made note of the location before slipping out of the shop and turning back toward the port. He needed to advise Nessa of this development.

They had found little in the way of leads on the origin

of the gunpowder, but there were signs of something more sinister in play. For one, no one seemed to know of the mystery airship or its crew. Admittedly, after he and his crew had taken the airship, he had given orders for the captain to be thrown overboard and the hostage pilots to be sent off with gliders, but he now questioned if Robbie had followed his instruction to spare them. Then again, there was no word of missing men either. It was a mystery that grew greater with each discovery. What had Robbie learned to inspire his mutiny? It must have been quite the offer.

He chose the stairs once he reached the base of the tallport. Thieves had taken to stalking the elevators at some of the less guarded docks, and he was in no mood to teach them a lesson today. The London airbours were a proper mess. Tallports had popped up across the sprawling city, and the Crown was only beginning to impose regulations on them.

They had chosen this dock as their temporary home in the east docklands through Tims' connections. It was sturdily built with good traffic, but not in the most lucrative area of town. The owner had longstanding arrangements with the local Tradist officials to be left to his own devices. His crew had stuck to targeting the outlying ports for their scheme, thinking it better to avoid the Tradist posts, but Clara would be pleased to learn of the ripe potential of the London docks if one knew whose palm to grease. He smiled to himself and made a mental note to ask Nessa to send the information along. The pilots who had journeyed to London with them had been busy, quietly picking up tithes from the less favoured merchants, befriending the local crews, right under the Tradists' noses with hardly any trouble.

The Captain Duke passed layer upon layer of airships until he came to his own, nodding to the pilot on watch and heading straight for his quarters. Nessa was in the office, looking over the latest missives and logbooks. He glanced at the built-in shelves that took up the corner. The books were neatly arranged, just as Clara had left them. He felt a pang of nostalgia and frowned. It had been hardly a fortnight since they left the Haven. And yet it seemed her presence in his thoughts grew with each day.

"Captain? You're earlier than I expected."

Startled, he shook his head to clear his mind and took a chair across from Nessa. The blonde pilot had ink smudged across her nose and her braid was uncharacteristically untidy.

"You look like you could use a break."

"Soon. Did you find the contact?"

"I was able to follow the man Alice spoke of, but I lost him in an alley off Brick St. It could be a meeting spot. Was Marie able to provide any assistance with the logs?"

"Yes, a great deal. In fact, I was about to leave a note. I'm joining her for dinner this evening and I was thinking we'd take another look together afterward."

"Ah, I see. You know, I hear most women prefer flowers to dusty old books."

"Marie is not most women," Nessa grinned. "I'll need to wash up before I leave. Could you take care of the latest missive to Reading?"

Her overly casual tone betrayed her intentions, and the Captain scowled. His narrowed eyes said she ought to leave the matter alone if she knew what was best. Naturally, she pressed the issue.

"What's happened?"

"Nothing."

"Really."

"She's quite busy I'm sure, there's no need to bother Clara with every little thing. There's nothing substantial to report. It can wait until your return."

"This is hardly some trivial thing. The crew is scattered to the four winds, it's crucial that we stay in contact with them."

"I am aware."

"So what is the real matter?"

The Captain shifted in his chair, his gaze fixed on the table, "We have not spoken since the Haven. She was… not pleased at being sent to Reading."

"Captain, the longer you wait, the greater the rift. A woman like Clara will not wait forever."

"Well, you're one to talk. How many years did it take for you and Marie to stop dancing around the issue?"

"That had its own complications, not to mention the fact she was still grieving her husband when I first met her. But look at us now. A proper courtship is what she deserves and it's what I plan to give her."

He sighed, "Fine. What advice would you give then? After all, we seem to share a taste for uncommon women."

"Tell her how you feel—or better yet, show her."

"And if she's decided she prefers a life in respectable

society?"

"Doubtful. You and Clara both display an impressive obstinacy when it comes to such things."

The Captain Duke rolled his eyes, "Clara is a lady of honour."

"Aye, and she fancies you. The honourable thing would be to take her at her word instead of making silly assumptions. Flowers, really." Nessa stood and stretched, gathering the books on the table.

Resigned, he took up position by the wireless. It was good to see Nessa so happy. She was positively humming as she took her leave. He read through the neatly composed notes and progress updates. Cat and Mouse seemed to be adjusting well to life in Reading, though there were scant details about Trick's recovery. The other crews were in fine form, and the black market network was holding strong thanks to Tims' careful machinations. The thought rose in his mind, as it had been wont to of late, that he had transformed into a figurehead. The work could likely continue with or without him, giving him an unfamiliar sense of liberation.

I could walk away from all of this.

But, just as quickly as it came to mind, the feeling was chased away by thoughts of his crew. He would not lightly give up the camaraderie and loyalty they had built together over the years. Still, their way of life was changing. They were adapting. And he dreamed his secret dreams of a future where their particular talents were not needed.

Nessa had waited for Marie. But it was less about the waiting and more that they each grew. They had grown into the people they needed to be for each other. Their strengths complemented each other. Together, they could be their true selves.

And perhaps that was the root of it. He had faint idea of who his true self was, and Clara too was caught between worlds. His commitment had been to his work and crew, and he had pushed concerns for his own happiness aside for so long that he hardly recognized it for what it was. Happiness. He had a chance to be happy and he was moping instead of reaching for it with both hands.

He preferred to let the rumours and legends define him, but it was not as though he lacked options. He had worn the guise of the Captain Duke for so long it felt odd to consider what might happen were he to take it off for more than a brief sojourn. With the seeds of an idea taking root in his mind, the Captain Duke bent to his task, transcribing Nessa's notes and adding his own for the missive to Reading. He would be ready, when they met again. He would be the man she needed him to be.

Chapter 12: In which our heroine remembers better days

The next evening, they were gathered for dinner at the house once again. Professor Sewell was nowhere to be seen, but Archie arrived with a note of apology, saying she was tied up with work but would join their party later. Clara gave him a curious look – he had been away all day and was still wearing the previous night's clothes – but he placed a finger to his lips before dashing up the stairs to shave and wash before the meal. He soon rejoined them wearing fresh clothing, though the dark circles beneath his eyes still spoke of a sleepless night.

Dinner proceeded at a snail's pace. Trick was quiet, though whatever the children had said to him the night before seemed to have lifted his spirits somewhat. And Archie's chef had outdone herself once more, with savoury soup followed by roast turkey and fingerling potatoes, warm rolls baked fresh that day with rosemary-infused butter, vegetables picked from the university's garden, and even some citrus on ice before the jellied desserts. Clara made a note to thank the kitchen staff. One could manage a dinner that lacked in either conversation or quality, but never both.

It was not until they had left the dining hall for coffee and tea that, as promised, the Professor arrived. She too had changed. Her dark hair was tossed back into a messy chignon, and there was yet a tell-tale smudge of grease highlighting her left cheekbone. She was followed closely by an assistant carrying a sizeable package. Any fears that the previous evening's events had caused irreparable offence were alleviated by her beaming smile as she went to Trick.

"Mr. Kilarney, I must beg your forgiveness."

"No, Professor, I am the one who must apologize. You have done nothing but try to help a sorry old man and I have been the most ungrateful wretch."

"No, please! It has been so long since my own injury, I had forgotten how unhappy it was. They told me I would never walk or run or dance again. As you can see, I proved them all wrong."

Professor Sewell gave a small pirouette before retrieving the package.

"I shall accept your apology only if you will do me the greatest honour and assist me in testing my latest piece."

With that, she lay the package in his lap. They gathered to watch as he removed the tissue wrapping, revealing a small case. As he opened it, a look of confusion crossed his face.

"I don't understand, what is it?"

"Another chance," she said softly. "May I show you?"

Archie came forward to help Trick remove his jacket. Professor Sewell fastened padding over the stump of his right arm, tucking in the seamed edge of the shortened sleeve, and buckled a harness around his shoulder. Finally, she attached the device, showing Trick how to fasten the clips as she worked. It was an unusual design, with straps that wrapped around his upper arm and a cone-shaped mechanism in place of his forearm, but no hand. Finally, she attached the final component to the delicate configuration of gears: a bow of the finest Pernambuco wood.

"Is that a Tourte?" he asked, in a tone of pure wonder.

"From our collection. But it deserves better than a dusty shelf, don't you think? There. Is that comfortable? Now you must try it."

Archie came forward bearing a violin, and after a moment's hesitation, Trick reached for it with his good hand. He stared at the instrument, and then looked about the room. Clara held her breath. She had never seen the veteran pirate so anxious, and wondered if he might run from the parlour. Then, Cat pulled a silver bracelet from her wrist, laying it on the small table beside him.

"I won't ask for Tammany's Jig just yet, but you'll owe me for next time."

And with that, Trick broke into a beaming smile, breaking the tension. Clara recalled her first feast aboard the airship, Trick with his accordion, accepting small favours in exchange for songs. She bit her lip to keep from laughing and pulled a ring from her finger to set it beside the bracelet. Mouse added a delicate autobauble from his pocket. Archie and Professor Sewell caught on quickly, adding their own tokens – a silk handkerchief, a small wrench. Trick stared at the growing pile, shaking his head. The room was silent as he touched the instrument, running the fingers of his left hand over the inlaid design. Then, he looked to Cat.

"Well, I can hardly refuse such a request."

Trick stood, flexing his arm as he tested the movement of the bow. The rest of them quickly found seats and watched with bated breath as he settled the violin against his shoulder. He placed the bow against the strings and drew it back, filling the room with a low hum. His next draw was not as successful; the bow slipped out of key and produced a jarring shriek. Trick winced, and paused, but took a breath and tried again.

Within minutes he had mastered the basic movements to place the bow as he wished, and the familiar opening bars of Tammany's came out, halting but recognizable. Clara could feel tears streaming down her cheeks. Mouse was clenching his sister's hand tightly, and she had put an arm around the boy. But the Professor's face was pure delight, and Archie was beaming beside her. Trick finished the song with his eyes closed, taking a deep breath before opening them.

"Well. This will do."

He looked to Professor Sewell, and she ran to envelop him in a hug.

"I cannot thank you enough," he said.

"That was the greatest thanks I could receive. Now, how was the tension? This is only a prototype, we wanted your input before we modified it further. I think we could shorten the bearing to improve the reach and still maintain the precision of the draw..."

Trick recovered his composure and soon was deep in conversation with the Professor over technical details and proper form. Archie came to stand by Clara, and she reached up to touch his arm.

"Thank you."

"Thank *you* for the idea. I should have thought of this long ago. His recovery will proceed nicely now, I think."

"I hope so. I fear our brief peace may not last long."

Her brother frowned.

"Clara, you know you may stay as long as you wish."

"It isn't quite so simple as that. I will not risk your safety and the security of this institution. There is important work being done here; you must not test the wrath of whatever or whomever is behind this intrigue."

"The university is not so vulnerable. There are powerful allies here, bound by a common vision to change the world for the better. I only ask you to consider what might be accomplished through more… legitimate means."

Clara opened her mouth to protest, but, not wanting to impede the goodwill of the evening, thought better of it. She took a breath and placed a hand on her brother's shoulder,

"I will consider it, though I make no promises."

Archie beamed, his smile growing as Professor Sewell came to join them, rattling off a list of alterations and enhancements she wished to make.

"I only hope I'll have enough time before I leave. Archie, you must help me with the blueprints; you have far more patience with the figures. I plan to stop by the London factory and I want to include this in the new designs."

"You're going to London?" asked Clara.

"Unfortunately, yes. Duty calls, and I expect it will be a dry affair. The Tradists have no sense of humour and I have no patience for their silly speeches, but they do have deep pockets."

"The Professor has a number of patents in production

for the Association of Merchant Traders; they're having a summit at the moment."

"And are calling me away from my work to attend the silly thing. I do wish you could join me, Archie."

"As do I, but I have lectures and I've already taken enough leave from my duties here. Clara, you have some… associates in London, perhaps you could provide some company."

"Yes!" said Cat, appearing at his elbow. "That sounds like a fine idea. Clara?"

"Cat, we must attend to Trick. I'm afraid the timing is simply not right."

"Get yourself off to London-town, I'm quite happy to stay," Trick said. "By the time you're back I'll have Tammany's Jig ready for ye."

"The timing could not be better. Leave the rehabilitation of Trick to me," said Archie. "I know you've been getting a touch of cabin fever here with us land-lubbers."

"Let me think on it," she said at last. "I'll write to Nessa at least."

Professor Sewell had her assistant fetch champagne for their little company, and they toasted to Trick's recovery and her continued success. The Kendrick Road house rang with sparkling voices, music and laughter late into the night.

Chapter 13: In which our hero confronts a captain

Nessa was in a dress, and she was not amused.

"This is why we picked up the debutante," she stage-whispered after escaping the over-enthusiastic shop girl.

"Clara cannot be responsible for all our ruses. Come now, you're doing a fine job."

"If I have to try on one more pair of— Oh, you've found the ivory silk. Hmm, this seems a little too colourless for my complexion, don't you think? Maybe a nice ecru, this time three-quarter length with a few more flourishes perhaps, yes?"

She waved away the girl as she pretended to inspect more of the glove shop's wares. The Captain Duke hid a smile, but kept his watch by the window of the store.

"How much longer do you think?"

"He's late. He usually comes out by a quarter after. Wait, look there!"

Their quarry was coming out from the alley, but this time he was not alone.

"The one with the bowler hat. That's the one who was lurking around that meeting point Robbie set."

Nessa narrowed her eyes, "There's something about the other one..."

"Miss?"

Startled, she turned about.

"Oh, the ecru. Yes, thank you. On second thought, I think I'll return with a sample of the fabric so we can match it precisely. Thank you ever so kindly, we will most certainly return post-haste, if you'll excuse us now we must be on our way."

Nessa gave a frightening smile to the poor girl, then, gripping the Captain's arm, she fled the store.

"I recognize him."

"Who?"

"His companion. Don't you? Well, you didn't nearly shoot the man I suppose."

"What? Who is he?"

"The captain of the gunpowder ship who damn near blew us into the heavens."

"It can't—I had him thrown overboard."

"You mean you ordered Robbie to."

The Captain Duke clenched his jaw. They continued to follow the two men at a reasonable distance, until they paused at the entrance to a pub. The one with the bowler seemed to console his acquaintance, and offered him a few coins, shaking his head. The former captain had his head bowed through the exchange, but accepted the money before entering the pub.

"Well, which should we follow?"

"I think we've found our source's source. Fancy a pint?"

"We may draw attention to ourselves, dressed up like this."

"It's a dress. You cut a fine figure, but rest assured, Ness, they're less likely to take note of a lass in a frock than one who looks as though she could take on the entire establishment—and win. No, I've a better plan."

Nessa entered the pub alone and approached the bar rail. Her target was already deep into his cups and did not notice until she stood at his elbow. Leaning in, she whispered into his ear.

"How far did you think you could run?"

Confronted by Nessa's steely gaze, the captain knocked his stool over in his haste to get away. Seeing her positioned between him and the entrance, he turned on a heel and fled through the kitchens and into the alley behind. She followed at a stately pace, arriving in time to see him pinned to the ground with the Captain Duke's knee at his back, his arm twisted behind him.

Nessa shooed the kitchen staff as she closed the door behind her, "Move along, move along, just a common ruffian. Nothing to see here."

Then, she turned back to their detainee.

"You. You remember me?"

He responded by spitting onto the ground. The Captain twisted his arm further and he yelped,

"Alright, alright! Yes, I remember you, wench. Just let me be."

"That depends entirely on how quickly you explain how a dead man is walking about before us. If I recall, you were about to take a dip in the channel."

"Aye, thanks to your scheming. You stole my ship! Twice! I should never have trusted the blond one."

The Captain Duke dragged him to his feet, "What do you know about Robbie Codswaddle?"

The man leered at them and Nessa realized the situation was getting out of hand.

"Now, now. There's no need for bloodshed," she said, taking out a handkerchief and pressing it to the man's bleeding lip. "Perhaps our interests in this matter align."

She traded a significant look with the Captain, and the man looked between the two of them, confused.

"Let's start with a name."

"Thompson," he replied.

"You see, Thompson, the blond man you dealt with, we're trying to find him too."

"So the hornswoggler is still alive? What of the cargo? Has he run off with it too?"

"He's run off, yes. What have you heard?"

"That's it, innit? Haven't heard a thing. He set up the meeting point and never showed. Figured he might be dead, or worse. Our benefactor is unhappy and soon I won't be able to show my face in any kind of company, respectable or not."

"So what are you doing in London?"

"I got word that the Admiral was 'ere, thought I could explain to him. I fought for 'im, I would have given my life for 'im. But with no goods to show, or coin to repay the man, I'm ruined."

He sighed bitterly and slumped. The Captain Duke could almost pity him. His dejection was complete. Nessa, however, was not so soft-hearted.

"Good to know. So now you're going to tell us exactly what you told Robbie to inspire him to abscond with your cargo, as well as its origins, or we're going to flag down the nearest Tradists and hand you over directly."

The man blanched, "Listen, I only know what I was told. The gunpowder had to get to London, and discreet. I don't know where it came from, I picked it up on the Isle of Wight with directions to leave that very night."

"And who was your contact there?"

"Uh, Corring. Alexander Corring. Military fellow, set to marry some fancy lass."

The Captain Duke felt a rush of anger.

"You had better not be lying to me," he said in a tone of quiet thunder.

"I'm not, I swear. Please, just let me be and I won't bother with any of this mess again. I swear it."

"What do you think, Captain? Is he a changed man? He does seem to have greater troubles than us."

"I already called for your life once, Thompson. You're too pathetic for a second attempt. If you think of anything useful, leave a note at this pub and we'll collect it. But, my colleague here is not so tender as I. Cross us again and there will be no such mercy."

Their former adversary looked to be near tears as he straightened his jacket and began to limp out of the alley.

"One more thing," said Nessa, as the man flinched. "Which Admiral?"

"Admiral Flint," said Thompson, before hurrying away.

The Captain Duke looked at Nessa, and grinned.

"I've missed that," she said. "Putting the fear in them."

"I think I have heard of this Admiral Flint. He's known to run in certain circles."

"Ah. Perhaps it's time for your 'friend' to return from his travels early."

"I was thinking the same. But what of the crew?"

"I'll handle it. Between our people and Marie's, we can cover your exit. We'll send word to Madge to set up a few sightings of a ginger Captain in the northwest."

"Good. Let's get back to the ship, I'll need to pack a new trunk."

Chapter 14: In which our heroine receives an unexpected guest

It was the day before Professor Sewell's departure when Mouse burst through the doors of the solarium, shouting for Clara. She jumped up from the settee where she had been deeply engrossed in a heavy tome on international trade agreements and swept back her skirts to pull a pistol from the hidden pocket Mrs. Cottingham had sewn into them, ready to take on whomever was threatening their hideout.

"Clara! Oh, you won't need that. It's Master Tims! He's here to see you! And he brought Lottie," he said.

The boy could hardly contain his excitement, breathless from running. Clara had just started to relax when a rather irate librarian appeared in the doorway.

"Now, young man, I will not have such tomfoolery in these halls—"

She paused, catching sight of her quarry, and Clara, armed with a shining pistol.

"Oh, it's not—" started Clara.

With a sigh, the woman fainted.

"Oh dear," said Mouse.

"Oh dear indeed. No running in the library."

"Yes, Ma'am."

Clara rolled her eyes, "Tims is here you say? Come, help me get her in a chair and let's be off before she wakes up. We'll explain it to the Professor later."

By the time they had crossed the wide expanse of lawn, the Professor was already at the base of the tallport, playing with a curly-haired tot who was operating a tiny wingding and running about as Cat stood at the side of Tims.

"Clara! She's charming. Such an inquisitive little soul. I'm so pleased you invited them to see our facilities."

Cat gave her a significant look.

"Ah, yes. I thought it would be a pleasant surprise before your trip," Clara said, as Lottie ran to envelop her in a hug.

"Where is Captain?" she asked, staring up with piercing blue eyes.

"Captain who?" asked the Professor.

"Oh, ah, a friend of ours," Clare began, before feeling a blush warming her cheeks.

"Lottie calls him captain because she's after his ship," Tims interjected, sweeping his daughter into his arms and plucking the wingding from the air as it whizzed by his ear. "We do appreciate the opportunity to visit. Clara spoke highly of your facilities and I thought it well to show Charlotte some of the world beyond my little workshop."

"Oh, of course! It is just so exciting to see an interest in the mechanicals at her age. Will you be staying long?"

"Only a day trip this time."

"Well then you must allow me to give you a tour," she said, beaming.

Tims set Lottie down to run ahead, and the little girl took the Professor by the hand, walking on the side of her shining prosthetic and peppering their stroll with a hundred questions. Clara smiled at the sight of them, the Professor answering each inquiry in language the child could understand.

"She'll learn a lot here, once she's old enough," said Tims, walking beside her.

"I think it's a fine institution for her future education, and I imagine she'll have a thing or two to teach them by that point. But I was not expecting you to make the whole trip out here just to see it. How is your wife?"

"She's doing fine today. Mrs. Cottingham is checking in. I would have sent word, but… well, I'll explain later."

Clara could hardly repress her curiosity, but the rest of the afternoon did not permit an opportunity for private discourse as they were led around by their hostess. Lottie proved to be quite the distraction for student and faculty alike as they made their way through the halls. It was not until after they had joined Archie and Trick for an early dinner that Professor Sewell took her leave, citing the need to finish packing for her journey the next morning.

Master Tims waited until the staff had cleared the room to pull an envelope from his inner pocket and handed it to Clara. It was a letter, an actual, physical letter. She quickly discovered the reason: the envelope also contained a drawing. A symbol that looked to be composed of some piece of equipment over a diagram of a heart. Clara studied the image, but soon turned to the letter to make sense of it.

"It's from Peg," she said aloud, passing the drawing to Trick.

"Why didn't she use the wireless?" asked Cat.

"Well, there's the drawing for one. She says she's concerned about messages being intercepted. That explains her cryptic tone of late."

"That's right," said Tims. "None of yours yet, I think. They don't know you're here and your crews keep on the move. I believe they need to be in range to get the signal."

"How did you discover this?"

Tims ran his hands through his sparse hair and leaned forward, "There were Tradist ships sighted last week near Keswick. They were headed in the direction of the Haven, so the next morning I took Lottie out for a flight around the Derwentwater and there are signs they landed there."

Clara said a silent thanks that they had taken all of the books and ledgers with them. There would be nothing for them to find except overturned furniture in the burnt out shell. She hoped they would think it abandoned.

"Next morning, some gentlemen came 'round my shop. There was nothing to find, but they made a few pointed inquiries. They flew off, but left a device of some sort at the post office, big antenna-like thing out the back, and ever since we've had trouble with our wireless. I had my suspicions, so I sent out a false call for a shipment the next eve in Whitehaven and had one of my contacts keep an eye out. Sure enough, the same bloody Tradists were prowling their docks that night. We've had to go back to airmail to coordinate our operations."

"How did he know they were one and the same?" asked Trick.

"There were some odd markings on the ship, and a few of them wore pins with that symbol there. Next a parcel comes in, hand delivered by one of yours from Peg's crew with that drawing. Said they've been seeing it at different ports and wanted to know if we had any information. I've sent word to my people to be extra cautious, but I wanted to get this to you myself straight away. I took the chance and used the university as a cover for our trip, to avoid suspicion. Everyone in the village knows Lottie is likely to come here one day."

"I'll pass on the warning to the crews. We'll need to come up with new codes in case they've cracked ours," said Cat.

"We have bigger problems than that, I think," said Trick.

"How do you mean?"

"It's unlikely they could have discovered the Haven without direction."

"Robbie? You think he would go to the Tradists?"

"I think the Tradists are far more involved in this mystery than we first suspected."

The table was quiet as his words sunk in. This was no simple case of smuggling. The Tradists had every means to import the gunpowder with all the protections of the empire. If they were resorting to illicit means…

Clara folded the letter and placed it back in its envelope, "I need to get this to the Captain."

"Professor Sewell leaves tomorrow; shall I send word that you'll be joining her?" Archie asked.

"Would she mind?"

"Not at all, she'll be delighted."

"Very well. Cat will be coming as well, I presume. And what of you, Mouse? Off on an adventure? Or will you be keeping Trick company here?"

They all looked to the boy, who fidgeted with a loose button on his sleeve.

"Well… Archie could really use my help I think…"

He looked to Clara's brother with a questioning look, as though seeking confirmation.

"Absolutely. Your work is incomparable. I'd be lost without your assistance," said Archie.

Mouse then looked to his sister, who seemed to be warring with herself but quickly replaced her frown with an encouraging smile.

"Yes, of course. We won't be gone long. And Trick still needs protecting."

That seemed to settle the matter, though both of the children looked concerned by the idea of their imminent separation. Clara wondered when last they had been apart, or if they ever were.

"Very well. Cat, send word to the crews. And Mouse, would you make a copy of this drawing? I'll take the original with me."

Mouse accepted the task with a beaming smile and left

to puzzle over it at a large writing desk in the corner. One of the revelations of their stay at Lovelace was the young boy's talent for technical drawings. No sooner had he and Archie conceived of a new design than Mouse had completed an illustration, with all of the mechanical intricacies. He had an excellent eye for detail, and patience – surprising for a boy of his age.

They said their farewells to Master Tims and Lottie before Trick escorted them to the tallport. Then Clara mounted the stairs to her rooms and began to pack her few belongings into a case. Archie followed behind and sat on the bed as she scowled at the jumble of clothing. Breeches and loose linen shirts were mixed with ruffled dresses and skirts. She sighed, picking up one thing and then another.

Her brother smirked, "Penny for your thoughts? Or is it a shilling?"

Clara smiled at their old joke. Their father had always instructed them to ignore the idiom and know the value of their minds. But that sent a fresh wave of nostalgia for her family and their home on the Isle of Wight. She struggled to keep her emotions in check, but her brother, ever the perceptive one, stood and put a hand on her shoulder.

"Hey now, what's this about? The last time you left there was nary a tear, and that was under far less certain circumstances."

Clara gave a rueful smile, "I was quite determined in my chosen course of action if you'll recall."

"And now?"

"I still am, it's only—it feels too soon to say goodbye once more."

"Clara, you can always return to us. Trick will be here as well, for the next stage of his treatment."

"Archie, you know I cannot. They need me. The university is lovely, but this is not my home."

"Where is home? The Haven is not safe. And you said so yourself, your scheme could be employed from anywhere. Why not Reading?"

"Because it—it just wouldn't work like that. We separated the crew out of necessity, but it cannot be that way forever. We need our Captain. We're stronger together."

Archie sighed, "I know I was a bit of a prat at first. But I've seen the way they look up to you, Clara. You have their respect and admiration." He took her hand, "I'm not trying to dissuade you from your new life. It was against my better judgement that I allowed you to persuade me to leave you on that airship, but you have thrived. I see that now. I just want you to have options."

Clara smiled, "I did not exactly plan to join up with a pirate crew."

"Yes, but that was different. Corring is not chasing you; he's too busy ducking his debtors. He'll not be mounting a challenge to us anytime soon. And these Tradists, well, I worry, Clara."

"Can you imagine me returning to the Isle, after all of this? Do the troubles find me or do I seek them out? If it's the former, then we would be no safer here. I cannot explain why I feel this way. I only know that I must see this through."

"Very well. Only consider my offer once this storm has

passed. Besides, mother will have my head if you don't start writing your own letters. I've covered for you long enough and I'll not be the one to tell her you've taken up with pirates."

"Do not trouble her! If she's enjoying France as much as you claim then there is nought to worry her about."

"Your secrets are yours to tell," he said smiling.

Clara set out her pilot clothes with her favourite deep purple overskirt, and quickly packed the rest for the next day's journey. She would miss the idyllic rhythm of their time at Lovelace, but she longed for the next adventure. She wanted to feel the wind brushing her cheeks and tangling her hair. She wanted rope and canvas bruising her ink-stained fingers once again. She knew her own heart, and it belonged to the sky.

Chapter 15: In which our heroine flies to a seabird lair

They were docked at The Royal, the finest of the London tallports. Six levels that stretched into the dense veil of fog that blanketed the city. Clara ran her fingers over the rail of the spoke as they crossed to the central tower, the structure inlaid with Her Majesty's coat of arms. She was not surprised by Professor Sewell's warm reception in the city. The woman was famous for her inventions, and although Clara knew she was driven by the science rather than profits, Georgina Jameson Sewell had done well for herself. After securing a promise to visit her factory the next day, the Professor departed to attend to her own business, leaving Clara and Cat to wait for their friends.

They had sent word ahead to Nessa of their travels, deciding the best course of action would be to have her meet them. The Royal was the safest tallport in the London airbours, and they dared not arouse suspicion by having the Professor take them to the docklands.

Finally, they saw the tell-tale blonde hair weaving through the crowds. She stood taller than half the men on the docks, and smiled above the crowd as she drew near.

"Ah, little Cat, I have missed you! Clara, welcome. You made it to London after all," Nessa smiled.

Clara laughed, realizing that notwithstanding a few

detours, her friend was right. They exchanged warm hugs amid the stares of curious onlookers. Nessa was dressed in her full pilot's regalia. Tight black trousers, with a supple leather vest fitted over her blouse. She had a strange mouthpiece hanging about her neck, a match to the goggles that rested on her head with exquisite detailing in jade.

"A gift, from Marie," she said, before handing two similar pairs to each of them.

"But what is it for?" asked Clara.

"You'll need it for where we're going. Come, I'll have the porters return for your things. Today, we fly."

Cat was bouncing with excitement as they traversed the docks, taking a plush, velvet-lined elevator to the upmost level of the tallport. The London particulate was thick at these heights, and Clara soon realized the masks were designed with some sort of filtration system. She breathed easier once it was securely fastened around her nose and mouth. Following Nessa's instructions, they strapped into the gliders waiting for them and walked to the end of a long tier. Clara felt a thrill run through her. It had been so long since they had flown freely.

Cat went first, showing off her innate ability by turning at the last moment to fall backwards off the spoke with a wave, twisting and banking around to glide above them. Nessa took a short run before launching herself into the aether, catching an updraft to soar upwards. Clara stood with her toes on the edge, feeling the straps of the glider hugging her body. With a smile, she pushed off, diving into the air as she revelled in the sensations. The wings caught a gust and she manoeuvered her way into a position behind Nessa. They made their way upwards, banking little by little without the benefit of the upper breezes, but soon burst through the oppressive haze into clear skies above. And there, the largest airship Clara had ever seen hovered over the city. A great ironclad vessel, with propellers that dwarfed the Captain Duke's galleon and a balloon that looked as though it could lift an entire city block.

Cat whooped with delight, weaving her glider in acrobatic turns around their party. Clara heard a shout from Nessa, and banked left to follow her as they climbed towards the rear of the ship. Soon she could see the landing platform and shadowed Nessa's movements to position herself. First was Nessa, who gracefully stepped onto the platform before clearing the way. Next was Clara's turn. Her approach was a tad too high to mimic her friend's poise. She caught a draft that pushed her sideways and her heart skipped a beat before she collapsed the glider wings and rolled onto the boards. A hand reached down to assist her, and she looked up into the face of Captain Marie Buchanan.

"That was well done for a first attempt," she said.

"Practice makes perfect," Clara replied with a smile.

Cat spun like a dancer as she retracted the wings and landed with her feet planted firmly on the deck, arms akimbo as she took a deep and gratifying sigh.

"And you must be the little Cat I've heard so many tales about," said Captain Buchanan.

Already flushed from the thrill of the flight, the girl blushed further at the attention.

"Captain Buchanan, it's an honour."

"The honour is mine. Welcome to the *Fregata*!"

The two gave the traditional pilot's handshake, grasping

each other by the forearm. After they'd all exchanged pleasantries, the group was escorted through the ship to a finely appointed room with enough chairs for all. Nessa took a seat next to Captain Buchanan.

"I was expecting the *Ariadne*, but this… I've never seen such craft!" said Clara, admiring their surroundings.

"My little *Ariadne* would not do for the storm season crossings. The *Fregata* can withstand all. In truth, I suffer in my abundance. So many ships in need of quality pilots," she replied with a sidelong smile at Nessa.

Clara grinned, pleased with the obvious affection the two had for each other. She supposed she ought to be shocked, but she knew that men held little attraction for her friend. The two were well matched, though Clara doubted even the great Captain Buchanan's abilities in luring Nessa away from their crew.

"Where is the Captain Duke? Will he not be joining us?" Clara did her best to keep the note of disappointment from her voice.

"His duties have taken him away for the time being," said Nessa, her expression suspiciously neutral. "At any rate, he has tasked me with filling you in on what we've discovered."

"Well, we have a lot to discuss," Clara replied, trading a look with Cat as she pulled the drawing from a hidden pocket.

Nessa studied the image, and the accompanying letter.

"Marie, you had better send for tea. This will be a long afternoon."

Hours later, Clara was pacing back and forth as they puzzled over the mystery. The gunpowder, her ex-fiancé, the Tradists, the strange symbol—what did it all mean? The intrigue grew with each discovery. It was clear they were dealing with no simple case of smuggling, but what was the motivation?

"It is not enough," she sighed. "There is still so much missing. How are we ever to figure out this entanglement?"

"Well, there is a chance we can learn more. Marie?"

"The summit this week is the culmination of the Tradist negotiations I've been attending to since my arrival in London. It is the informal meetings where the real decisions are made, however. There will be a salon the day after tomorrow. Unfortunately, I have not been able to secure an invitation, but," she paused, "We understand the professor you travelled with is well regarded by their company."

"Professor Sewell? Oh, of course. Let me speak to her, I'm certain arrangements can be made."

Marie and Nessa exchanged a look.

"Have you told her of the gunpowder? Of any of this?" asked Nessa.

"No. Archie knows, but he thought it best to keep the university uninvolved. He's quite protective of her."

"Negotiations are somewhat fraught around the changing nature of international trade. Some are arguing for open borders, others for strict adherence to colonial boundaries. But tensions are growing between the factions and I do not know where your professor falls in all of this. I think it best to avoid mention of the true nature of your visit, if possible."

"I was not planning to. However, I must say that Professor Sewell has been nothing but gracious and kind to us. She's helped Trick, Ness. He played for us. There was a time I thought he might never smile again, yet there he was, laughing."

"That may be so, but we must be careful, Clara. I was as glad to hear of Trick's progress as you, but we must not let it cloud our judgement."

"Nessa, she is a friend."

"Not all friends can be trusted," she said, with bitter recrimination in her eyes. "Have we not learned?"

Clara felt the flush growing on her neck, "Robbie's betrayal hurt us all. But we cannot let it harm our ability to see the good in people. I have seen nothing but her sincere motivation to better the world through her inventions."

"I believe you," Captain Buchanan interjected, laying a hand on Nessa's arm to silence her protests. "But for all our sakes, we must be cautious. If you are right, we would not do well to draw Professor Sewell into this quagmire. And if you are wrong, we are left vulnerable to exposure. Think of your crew. Think of Master Tims and those who risk their lives and livelihoods to ensure the common people receive a decent meal. I've heard tales of your cleverness, Clara, but it is ruthless intelligence that will keep your loved ones safe in this place."

The room was thick with silence. Clara struggled with her desire to defend her optimistic perspective, but it clashed with her respect for the two women and their far greater experience of the world.

"I like Professor Sewell, but I don't trust her."

Cat spoke up from her position in the corner of the room. She was perched on a chest of drawers, with a plate of exotic fruits beside her, procured by Marie's pilots who held a soft spot for the pirate girl.

"What do you mean?" Clara asked.

"She sees the world as a problem to fix. Think of it. Archie is well matched to her because he reminds her we're human. But she needs to be reminded."

Clara made to dismiss such a ridiculous claim, but her brow furrowed as she recalled how her brother had been the one to explain Trick's anguish to the inventor.

"In any case," Captain Buchanan spoke. "We do need her help. Good intentions or not, she is a friend and valuable ally. Clara, I will respect your judgement on this matter, but I would advise patience before revealing our secrets."

"Your advice is welcome. I will wait until we know more. I will ask her, though, about the salon. I don't foresee any problems gaining entry for our party."

"Excellent. Then, shall we dine? It is nearing the supper hour, you must join us."

Cat hopped off the chest—the growing girl ever eager for a good meal—and they set off to join the pilots in the mess hall. The *Fregata*'s rooms were surprisingly cozy for an airship of such size, but Captain Buchanan explained how the bulk of the ship's space went to the cargo holds. Named for a seabird that could soar for days on the wind currents of the Caribbean, the airship was built to withstand months in flight without the need to resupply. It was not until after the meal that Nessa and Clara found a moment to speak alone, while Cat and Captain Buchanan explored the upper decks.

"I am sorry if I caused offence earlier. I have not met the Professor. I should not be so quick to judgement."

"No, your instincts are correct. We do need to be careful, there are too many unknowns. I wish the Captain was here. If he met her…"

"He will be away for some time I think."

"How could he leave at a time like this?" she asked, aware that disappointment rang in the tone of her voice.

"He felt it necessary."

"But the crew! Trick! What could possibly be more important than this?"

Nessa smirked, and went to the rail, staring out over the darkening city.

"I told him you would be unhappy."

"I—what? Well, of course I am."

"Because of the crew."

"Yes, because of the crew. Why else?"

Nessa only smiled, "I think there's someone you should meet."

"Who?"

"He's… a friend."

Nessa pulled a small notebook and pencil from her

pocket and wrote down an address, folding it and handing it to Clara,

"He'll have the answers you seek."

Curious, Clara tucked the note into her pocket. Their conversation was interrupted by the return of Cat, jubilant over her tour. Captain Buchanan was teasing Nessa, saying she would steal the budding pilot away from the Captain Duke. This seemed to be an ongoing exchange between the two. If Nessa ever decided to turn legitimate, she had a wealth of opportunities waiting for her.

It struck Clara, that she was so committed to the Captain Duke and their crew she would forfeit such a prospect. But Nessa cared for her work, and it looked as though the affection she shared with Captain Buchanan had sustained itself for years while they were apart. It was as likely to last as any partnership. Clara envied the ease they shared in each other's company. The deep respect for one another's chosen path and profession. They returned to the Captain Duke's airship in the docklands that night. Clara retired early, citing tiredness from the day of travelling, but nursing an inner turmoil of unknown origin.

Chapter 16: In which our heroine courts a gentleman

Clara checked the address twice before mounting the steps to knock on the door of a grand old house. It was a fine neighbourhood, not the most fashionable quarter but a perfectly respectable area. A big, brass knocker announced her presence. She questioned whether she ought to have changed her clothes, but she had flown to call on Professor Sewell that morning, and had not thought to bring an afternoon gown.

First they had visited one of the factories working to produce the Professor's inventions. Their tour was brief, but the facilities had left an impression. Row upon row of diligent workers, hard at work piecing together the molded metals. The foreman oversaw the operation, walking the length of the hall on a contraption of four spindly legs that lifted him to the height of two men. He had lost both of his own legs while fighting the Boers. Professor Sewell had spoken at length of her desire to see the workhouses empty and the impoverished gainfully employed. Part of the factory was set aside for schooling, offering a free education to the children and siblings of her employees with a focus on mathematics and the foundational study of biomechanical engineering.

They had drawn stares at the hotel where they shared a meal with other scientists; word of the Professor's visit had evidently spread. There, Professor Sewell said she was more than happy to include Clara's friends in her entourage for the next evening's salon, and, with a twinkle in her eye, had been effusive in her insistence that Captain Buchanan join them.

Clara's last errand was to visit the mystery address. And so, she straightened her jacket and assumed her most charming smile for the butler who answered with a scowl.

"Hello, I'm looking for—"

"The master of the house is not at liberty to receive visitors," he said, looking her up and down before shutting the door.

Clara frowned, and knocked again, louder. The butler peered out through a crack.

"If you would be so kind, sir, I am only in town for a brief visit and I would be ever so grateful if you would inform your master that I wish to speak with him."

"And you are?"

"Clara… Whittington," she said after a pause. Then with a tilt of her chin, "Lady Clara Whittington."

The butler shrugged and moved to close the door once more.

"Wait, I—Tell him I was sent by the Captain Duke!"

He paused, considering her. Clara gave up the niceties and placed a hand on the door.

"It is of critical importance that I speak to your master, today."

She injected her stare with all the gravity she could

muster.

"This is a respectable household; I'll have no talk of pirates upsetting him."

Clara stood firm.

With a grandiose sigh, the butler opened the door, "Very well, you'd better come inside."

He hurried her into the foyer, setting the latch before leading her down the hall at a brisk pace. He shoved her into a large library with a harsh whisper to stay put before disappearing back into the house. Clara let out her breath in a huff and explored the room.

Tall shelves stretched upwards to meet the high ceiling, framing a large window. Two large, wing-backed armchairs were placed near the fireplace, giving the room a cozy feel. She crossed to pick up a book that had been left on the side table, but froze as she reached for it. *The Press and the Public Service* by Grenville-Murray, the very book she had given to—

The door opened behind her and she whirled around to see—

A man, dressed in the latest fashion of the continent, waistcoat and all, bright red hair combed back into a tidy plait. He was wearing spectacles. And he was working quite hard to show no recognition under the disapproving eye of the butler.

"Master Olivier, this young woman has come here with the notion that you have information regarding that dreadful pirate captain."

"Ah," said the man with a perfectly posh accent. "Has

he offended you in some way?"

"He's about to," said Clara with narrowed eyes.

The Captain Duke barely hid his smirk before turning to his servant, "Would you please allow us some privacy, Sebastian?"

"Sir, I— Of course, sir," he acquiesced, glaring at Clara before closing the door.

"Olivier?" she asked once they were alone.

"My name."

"Your name is Olivier?"

"My family's name, actually."

"Your family name?"

"Yes."

"So…"

"Marmaduke. Marmaduke Ivan Lysander Olivier."

Clara stared. The transformation was remarkable. Gone was her wild pirate captain with his tangled locks and eyes full of mischief. In his place there was… a gentleman. She walked over and removed his glasses, peering through them at the nearest set of shelves. False, as she suspected. She set them aside and looked him in the eyes. Still full of mischief.

Finally, she smiled, "I suppose we both have our secrets then."

"I was going to tell you."

"How long have you been here?"

"Four days."

"Why?"

"I have some contacts here I wanted to check in with. And so, Olivier has returned early from his travels this year. Sebastian is quite out of sorts over my sudden reappearance. I do apologize for his behaviour."

Clara took a breath while she considered this revelation. She could feel her heart fluttering in her chest as she tried to sort through her emotions. She had missed him, yes, but to see him so unexpectedly... She felt nervous, and elated; it was strange to see him in the trappings of her previous world.

"Take your hair down," she demanded.

"My—why?"

"I like it better that way."

He grinned at her forwardness, "Sebastian will give me hell."

Clara raised an eyebrow, and the Captain Duke reached back and undid his hair, shaking it out into its usual tangle.

"Better?" he asked.

Clara ran her thumb over the embroidered waistcoat, and pulled him closer. It amused her, this reversal. Now she was the pirate queen, courting her gentleman suitor. She smiled as she drew him into an embrace. Oh but she had missed him, missed his warmth and the brush of his lips on her own. She let herself be carried away by the kiss, feeling his strength as he wrapped his arms around her, lifting her to her toes as he pressed against her. When they finally broke apart he picked her up and spun in a circle, laughing. She felt as though they had tipped over the edge of some great precipice. Only instead of falling, she felt as though she could float on thin air. There was so much she wanted to say, but dared not speak of… not yet at least.

"What shall I call you then?"

The Captain Duke's lips parted in surprise, "I hadn't thought of that."

"Well, if I continue to address you as Captain dear Sebastian might take offense. Trick must know, and Nessa and Marie. What do others call you? Just Olivier?"

"Some."

"Marmaduke?"

He made a face and Clara laughed.

"Trick uses it on occasion. He's the one who came up with my nom de guerre. Captain Marmaduke did not have quite the same effect."

"So… a pirate by trade, and what? A scholar? The storm season—you must come here for the winter months. You collect so many things on your travels, it's perfect, really. How do they not guess?"

"Few have ever made the connection. They think I'm quite bookish. Rumours of a family connection, but I do my best to quell them." He gave her a roguish look, "I find launching into a tale of how my distant ancestor made the acquaintance of Grace O'Malley tends to bore them into complacency."

"Did they?"

"Did who?"

"Did your family know Grace O'Malley?"

"Perhaps. There's some Irish on my mother's side I believe."

"Your parents…?"

"Long since deceased."

"I'm sorry."

"It's no matter."

"So you had a perfectly normal upbringing? None of the stories are true?"

He gave her a roguish smile, "Well some of the stories are true. But as for my parentage, just your average child out of wedlock I suppose."

"Ah. Your father, he was a noble?"

"My mother, actually. Noble by birth, a countess by marriage. My father was a good man, a tradesman. He did his best by me. It wasn't until my mother passed that I received all of this," he said, gesturing about the room.

Clara wanted to know more, but she didn't feel it appropriate to press for details just now. There were other matters at hand and she had so much to tell him. So, she wrapped her arms around his waist and pulled him in for a long, lingering kiss.

"What was that for?"

"For luck. We have work to do."

"Oh?"

"We're going to a party thrown by friends of the Tradists tomorrow night. The Professor has secured invitations, but my name will make it difficult to snoop. Cat is scouting the layout and talking up the caterers, but of course we'll need to make arrangements for you—"

"There's no need."

"I beg your pardon?"

The Captain Duke picked up an envelope, heavy and embossed with gold leaf detailing.

"I already have an invitation."

"An invitation?"

"Yes."

"To a salon. You attend salons."

"On occasion."

"This is how you know so much about the Tradists. Olivier is…"

"Olivier is an eccentric traveller, quite entertaining at dinner parties and the like, ever the gentleman but a tad academic for the likes of the Tradists," he said, as he collected the discarded spectacles and hunched his shoulders in a bookish slouch. "Still, he rounds out the table nicely and is usually adept at conversing on current affairs."

Clara smiled. She was going to be fond of this Olivier character.

Chapter 17: In which our hero finds himself in polite company

The salon was to be held at the residences of Mrs. Branson-Honeycutt, a hostess with a taste for robust intellectual discourse and little patience for politicking. Her guests were ever at the mercy of her sharp wit and sharper tongue, but the Captain Duke had made a significant effort to ingratiate himself with the woman and her circle of elite logicians and artists.

He took an hors-d'oeuvre from the autobauble-waitron as it wobbled through the assembled company. Tonight, the theme was the Mechanical World, and the guests had outfitted themselves accordingly. Decorative gears adorned their top hats and sashes. Pocketwatches of the latest fashion were displayed with glass backing so as to show off the delicate mechanisms within. Richly-coloured fabrics were trimmed in brass and gold, and the ladies wore jeweled cogwheels in their tightly-curled hair. The Captain was quickly drawn into conversation about the latest developments in Austrian aeronautical design, but all discussion was halted when the famed genius made her entrance.

Professor Georgina Jameson Sewell wore a cream gown with gold trim, the skirts swept back to reveal her gilded limb. The hush that befell the room turned to whispers as her entourage was announced. The murmur grew to a buzz over the three women, their presence dominating the room.

Captain Marie Buchanan — the Black Widow herself! — had her long locs in an elegant updo, clad in a fine yellow gown that was trimmed and tucked to the latest Parisian designs. Nessa was outfitted in a suit of grey, cut to flatter her figure and height, complete with a matching yellow pocket square. Her pale blonde hair was pulled into an elaborate braid that hung to the small of her back. The pair made a handsome couple to be sure. But the Captain Duke was struck speechless by their companion. Clara had found herself a gown of the latest fashion, borrowed, perhaps, from the Professor, as the amethyst bodice bared her shoulders, and the overdress was drawn up to reveal sheer skirts of lilac silk beneath.

While the Professor was quickly drawn into a knot of learned gentlemen, the assembly seemed content to levy their naked curiosity without engaging directly with the strange trio. But Mrs. Branson-Honeycutt was an old hand, both in securing the most noteworthy guests for her soirees, and in ensuring that all felt welcome in the space. Gossips would find themselves without future invitations, and cliques were broken with a subtlety that would have shamed her Majesty's finest diplomats. Flaunting her triumph at securing what would certainly be the most discussed guest list of the autumn, she glided towards the group and began to escort them about the room, making introductions as necessary.

A flash of Clara's expression of delightful mischief was all it took to set the Captain Duke's heart racing. Seeing his opportunity, he positioned himself at the elbow of Mrs. Branson-Honeycutt while the pilots were busy conversing.

"Madame, you are aware, I hope, of my extreme gratitude for your benevolence, inviting me as you do to these legendary evenings."

"Master Olivier, it is ever our pleasure to have such a prolific traveller in our midst. The rosewood cigar box you sent in the spring was simply exquisite. And I've told you, it's Dottie to my friends."

"A mere token, Dottie. For I do believe I will find myself even greater in your debt."

"Oh?" replied the matron, her interest piqued. "Do tell."

"I must admit to an infatuation."

"Olivier! You never allow me to meddle in your romances—or lack thereof. Tell me what has brought on this change of heart and how I may encourage it?"

"The young lady there, in the violet. I must know her name, or I shall spend the rest of my days a besotted fool."

He was trusting in her nature as a true romantic, but with one shrewd glance, he was reminded that Mrs. Branson-Honeycutt was no easy mark.

"Your prose is purple, but your heart, I think, is true," she said, before grabbing him by the elbow and steering him into the circle. "Her ladyship is the only daughter of the late Baron Whittington, a fine family, well-connected. Not a hereditary title, of course, but all the same she is said to have a generous allowance..."

A young man had made the error of attempting to impress Clara with his paltry knowledge of global relations. She was in the act of dismantling his credibility with masterful incisiveness.

"By way of Denmark, you say? I believe the cattle in that region were of Dutch origin."

He sputtered, "Ah, well, one and the same, to be sure. They must be from Holstein."

"Hardly, I should think. Particularly after Schleswig."

Mrs. Branson-Honeycutt chose that moment to rescue the fumbling fool.

"Lady Whittington! Did I hear correctly that you are recently returned from France? Our Master Olivier is an unrepentant explorer himself, ever leaving our quaint company for far-flung adventures."

Face to face, it was hard to hold the dispassionate expression he usually adopted on such occasions. Particularly when confronted by the coquettish look in her eyes.

"Master Olivier, what is your opinion on the state of diplomacy with the continent?"

The Captain Duke smiled, "I find it best to adhere to the experts in these matters. Too often I find that our brightest applicants to the diplomatic trade are turned off by the promise of a penniless existence in the least favoured missions. It is of the utmost importance in our current day that these appointments be based on merit over aristocratic heritage."

"Grenville-Murray makes a compelling argument for the modernization of the diplomatic service, does he not?"

"I recently obtained a copy of *The Press and the Public Service* from a cherished friend, and I must admit I am absolutely riveted by its contents."

The other man gave a fretful laugh, "The reporter? The Roving Englishman? Hardly an authority I would think."

"Oh, you've read him?" asked Marie with an expression of innocence.

"I—no, I have never found myself afflicted with bookishness. I speak of the world as I see it."

"Ah. That explains it," she said, turning her attention back to Nessa.

Unsure of whether an insult had been made at his expense, he soon found reason to seek refreshment on the other side of the room. Mrs. Branson-Honeycutt had a twinkle in her eye as she left the Captain Duke in the company of Clara, Nessa and Marie.

"Splendid turnout, is it not?" asked Captain Buchanan.

"Marie, Marie, you'll never make friends if you provoke them so," said Nessa with a smile.

"We did not come to make friends; we came for information."

"She speaks truth," said Clara. "Shall we mingle?"

"That was the plan," he smiled. "Speaking of which, what have you done with Cat?"

The Captain Duke looked about the room, but could see no sign of the girl. Then, a young man appeared at his elbow with a serving tray of sparkling wines. Apparently the waitron was too unstable to trust with fine glassware. It took a second look and a tell-tale giggle on Clara's part before he recognized her under the slicked-back hair and suit. A false mustache graced her upper lip, and her recent growth spurt had sharpened her cheekbones, lending credence to the illusion.

"At your service, Captain!"

They all accepted a glass and toasted to the success of their mission of discovery before dispersing throughout the room, keeping a watchful eye on the guests and notables.

The Captain Duke found reason to stay by Clara's side. Her knowledge of social graces was exemplary, and she spoke with an ease that made him ever aware of the difference in their stations. But her subtle flirtations were met and matched by his own familiarity with courtly graces, and he relished the opportunity to lavish his attention on such a deserving subject. The brush of her skirts, the rose bloom on her cheeks, the sparkle in her eye as she looked up at him. They were soon the talk of the room. He had begun to feel a sense of destiny, that although he had assumed his natural identity as Olivier for strategic purpose, it may come to pass that his dual life could be the means by which he and Clara could be together.

His optimism grew as the evening passed, the hours counted by uncorked bottles. But the Captain did notice when, as the hour grew late, Professor Sewell slipped away from the room in the company of a silver-haired gentleman of military bearing. His curiosity piqued, he excused himself from their group with a significant look to Clara, and followed them into the hall.

The two were deep in conversation as they walked, crossing into a second passage that led to an antechamber. It was not until the Professor began to reach for a light fixture that the man turned and caught sight of the Captain.

"You there! What are you doing here?"

"Oh, beg pardon, I thought you were headed to the gentleman's lounge. Is this not the way?"

"It is not."

"Oh. My apologies!"

He made as if to leave, and caught the two sharing a look. Turning back, he cocked his head as though he had only just noticed the woman in their midst.

"Say, aren't you the Professor Sewell I have heard such high praise about?"

"Yes, that would be me."

"Professor, I must thank you!" he said, crossing the space to clasp her hands. "I heard of your work tonight with an acquaintance of mine. A talented musician, one of Britain's finest!"

"Oh, Master Kilarney!" the Professor said, warming to his company. "Yes, our work with him is seeing great progress. The prototype is functioning quite well – he played for us just this week. I shall tell him of your interest in his recovery, Mr.—?"

"Olivier. Thank you. That is the most excellent news. And you are?" he asked, turning to the frowning man who glowered at their familiarity.

"Oh, this is Admiral Flint. Forgive his moodiness, it's only his nature."

The admiral narrowed his eyes, but pasted a smile on his lips and extended a hand to the Captain Duke.

"Thank you for your interest. Now, if you'll excuse us, Professor Sewell and I have business to attend to."

"Ah, of course," he said with a bawdy wink. "Pleasure to meet you both."

With no other choice, he noted the location of the passage and returned to the party. Resuming his position at Clara's side, he waited for a quiet moment to share his discovery. But just as they finished conversing with a long-winded author about his latest work on the nature of humankind in the aeronautical era, a hush fell as an impressively mustachioed man escorted a golden-haired and visibly pregnant woman into the room and the guests dipped into a mixture of bows and curtsies. The royals had arrived.

Chapter 18: In which our heroine makes an indecent proposal

The salon was well attended, and populated with all manner of notable personages. The erudite and the industrialist alike waxed poetic over the delicate treats carted around by a mechanical waitron. Artist and inventor conspired to dream up the most delightfully impossible things. Clara was heartened to see such collaboration among the finest minds of the nation. It was a far more exciting affair than she had anticipated, and she found herself swept up in the enchantment of the ideas that flowed as freely as the wine.

Their arrival had caused a stir, but it was the Captain Duke's reaction that pleased her most. He stared at her with mischief in his eyes, contriving a formal introduction and attending to her as any suitor would. He was dressed in a finely cut suit with his hair pulled back in a low plait that made her long to see it tumbling and loose again. But here, in this space of enforced propriety, she had license to pursue him as she wished.

Her lessons in etiquette under the watchful eye of Miss Ellington had included training on all the subtleties of courtly flirtations, and she was employing them shamelessly tonight. A sidelong glance, a brush of the hand. They orbited each other, two suns converging and lending their brightness freely to all in their midst. The gaiety of the salon was infectious. She had almost forgotten their original purpose when he left her side to trail the Professor.

She caught a wink from Nessa, who crossed the room to join her with Marie on her arm. Amidst the mixed company of artists and idealists, they were far from the most unconventional pairing, and the two had embraced the opportunity to display their affection for one another without reserve.

"Enjoying the evening?" Clara asked as they drew near.

"Quite so," Captain Buchanan replied with a smile. "You appear to be having quite the time yourself. Where is your besotted escort? He has hardly left your side."

"Shocking, is it not? How terribly inappropriate we are tonight."

"Propriety is overrated," said Nessa, raising her glass.

They moved on to the next clutch of Tradists, teasing out tidbits of information from the inebriated and overconfident. The most level-headed guests vacillated between cautious appraisal of the proposal for greater collaboration between states and concern over the shift from the colonial borders. Many showed far greater concern about the state of their investments than for protecting the lower classes during the next great economic shift.

Just as the Captain returned, the room was taken by the arrival of the Princess and Prince. They paid their greetings to the hostess, and before she could ask the Captain what he had learned, the woman caught sight of Clara. With a beaming smile she waddled across the room, voluminous skirts doing little to disguise her state of gravidity.

"My dear Clara, how wonderful! I had not thought to see you again until our return to Osborne."

"Your Royal Highness, it is good to see you," she said as she dipped into another curtsy. "And in such good health! Surely your confinement must begin soon."

"Quite so. Mother insists we stay at Windsor for it. We leave for Berkshire in three days' time."

"That is happy news. It makes my heart glad to see you so."

"And you as well! Ah, Henry. You remember Lady Clara?"

The prince joined them, his arm placed protectively at his wife's back.

"From our wedding, of course. I was so sorry to hear of your father's passing. He is greatly missed."

The pang in her heart was quickly subsumed by gratitude for their remembrance of her father. She gave her thanks, and the couple were soon drawn away by other dignitaries, but not before securing a promise from her to visit after the birth of their child.

The Captain Duke turned to her, "You attended the wedding of the Princess Beatrice?"

"Of course, last summer."

"Of course."

"Yes. The Royal family stays quite frequently on the Isle of Wight. Her Majesty prefers it."

"Oh?"

She smiled. Life on the Isle of Wight had a different pace from the formalities of London.

"My brother and I have no titles of our own, only well-connected relations. My grandmother was a countess and waited on Her Majesty. But with no male heirs, the family title was passed to a distant cousin," Clara explained. "My father, for his service, was given a baronage for life. Princess Beatrice had many duties but she enjoyed our company, so my father would bring us to visit now and then. She would stage these wonderful tableau vivants at Osborne."

He shook his head, smiling, "You lead an interesting life, Clara Whittington."

"One day I shall compel you to finish telling me of yours, Marmaduke Ivan… Olivier."

"Lysander," he corrected with a laugh.

"Marmaduke Ivan Lysander Olivier." She cocked her head, "Milo, then. That shall be it."

"Milo?"

"M-I-L-O. Milo."

"You may call me whatever you wish," he said, moving closer.

Clara bit her lip and leaned slightly forward until their forearms touched. The barest contact, and yet it sent her heart racing. She saw his breath catch, and the longing in his eyes had her craving his touch.

"Captain, if we do not remove ourselves from polite company I am about to do something indecent."

"Clara! I…"

"I believe Nessa will be returning to the *Fregata* this evening. I'll have them drop me off at the docklands on the way. Meet me, at the airship. Tonight."

With a smile, he took her hand and pressed a kiss to her palm.

"My lady, it would be my pleasure."

She could not help the blush that rose to her cheeks, but she was ignorant of the stares they received. The wild captain, the scholarly gentleman, both stood before her in one man.

"We must leave separately, or we'll cause an even greater stir."

"A pity, or I would fly you away this very moment."

"I'll see if Nessa and Marie are ready to leave. Check in with Cat before you go, she's planning to stay on with the staff and will meet with us tomorrow."

"Giving me orders, Quartermaster?"

"Here, I outrank you," she smiled.

Clara pressed her hand into his once more before they parted. She could not help her blush as she joined her friends.

Chapter 19: In which our hero errs in his judgement

The Captain Duke went in search of Cat, but none could recall having seen the "young man" for the past hour. The salon was winding down. Mrs. Branson-Honeycutt held court in the parlour as her royal guests listened politely to a young lady espousing her philosophy on the importance of enfranchisement of women voters. He searched the balcony and the hall for another half hour before making his way to the library near the antechamber. He pretended to peruse the extensive collection, fending off solicitations to discuss the latest plays of the west end, before he heard voices in the hall.

Positioning himself in the shadow of the arched door, he watched as a company of a half dozen men passed by, boisterous in their good cheer. Professor Sewell was with them, Admiral Flint at her side. She seemed pleased, though it was hard to tell from their backs as they continued their progress and turned a corner.

The Captain made his way down the passage they had come from, examining the lamp in the antechamber. He looked about him and gave the fixture a tug. Nothing. He considered it for another moment before giving it a twist. A panel slid noiselessly aside to reveal a room. He had barely stepped across the threshold when a shape sprung at him, spinning him backwards before the panel closed once more with a thud. Breathing heavily, Cat stood before him in the antechamber, looking as though she had seen a spirit.

"Sorry, Captain. I managed to sneak in, but I couldn't find my way out. How did you find me?"

"By chance it seems. What have you learned?"

"I got in earlier when we were setting up the room and hid. Seemed like this was where all the bigwigs would be coming. And I was right. But Captain, the Professor was here. Her inventions, they're using them to build an army."

"Well, that makes sense. Her military connections are well known."

"No, Captain. An army. Not Her Majesty's forces, the Tradists. A faction of them at least. They want their own, private army. I can't remember all of it, but they mentioned the missing gunpowder, and needing a different kind of distraction to encourage support from the people, and the Crown. They want people to be afraid."

"Did it sound as though they would act soon?"

"They spoke about a demonstration of some kind. They didn't go into details."

"Professor Sewell is involved?"

"They were asking her about her inventions and complaining of the stalled talks at the official meetings. The Professor seemed awfully familiar with the Admiral. They must be friends. I can't be certain, but she did say she had plenty of models ready for examination at their leisure. It would be during her visit here; within the week, I imagine."

"We must get word to the others. Take my glider, go to Nessa and Marie on the *Fregata* and tell them everything.

Send word to your brother and Trick. I'll see to Clara."

The little pilot left, and the Captain Duke had been forced to make his way by other means. The mechanicab was painfully slow as it moved through the streets on the way to the docklands. The Captain Duke wished for the hundredth time that he had brought a spare glider. As they drew closer, his heavy heart began to lift. Whatever mess they had found themselves in, they would find a way through it, together.

As the mechanicab pulled up to the tallport, he looked up to find his airship among the many tiers.

In the light spilling from the windows of his cabin, he could see her figure pacing the room. Grinning like a besotted fool, all was forgotten. The bad news could wait a little while, he thought, as he tossed some coin into the front of the cab and hurried to reach the central tower. He briefly considered the stairs, spiralling upwards, before seeking out the elevator. He tapped his foot as he watched it descend, stopping at each tier on its way down.

He felt nervous—giddy, even—his mind consumed by thoughts of what to say. Or if anything needed to be said. He just wanted to see her, to be in her company forever. A kiss, he decided, spoke volumes.

The doors opened, but before he could step inside, a small noise alerted him that he was no longer alone. He ducked the first punch, but found himself surrounded by three men of the vilest sort. He downed two of them before a fourth came from behind. Blows rained upon him and the world fell to black. His last thought was of Clara as he felt himself being bound and carried away.

Chapter 20: In which our heroine dreams

Clara hummed as she paced the length of the room, enjoying the feeling of her skirts swishing around her ankles. The gown she'd borrowed from Marie fit like a dream. She gave a little twirl and watched as the lilac fabric flared with the movement, vowing to have Mrs. Cottingham make her another. There could be future occasions for such dress, she thought, smiling to herself. Best to be prepared.

The airship was tranquil, floating high above the city, no rumbling carriages to disturb the peace. Clara yawned, fighting the sleepiness that threatened to overcome. She sat on the bed, looking to the timepiece the Captain kept on the little desk in the corner. It was quite late, nearing 2'o'clock in the morning.

Just for a moment, she thought, as she lay down and closed her eyes.

Falling into her dreams with a smile, certain she would soon be woken with a kiss, Clara slept.

Stay tuned for the thrilling finale in Book 4!

Tales of the Captain Duke:

Of Tempests and Teacups

rebeccadiem.com

Bonus: The Adventures of Cat and Mouse #1

A short story first featured in the October 2015 edition of Airmail

Catherine Waugh searched her bag for the last of the biscuits and came up with crumbs. She took a deep breath before uncorking the water flask and turning to her brother with a smile.

"Here you are! Just enough to wet your whistle."

She dribbled some into Morris' open mouth. He giggled and most dribbled down his chin. For the hundredth time that morning, Cat reminded herself that a toddler could not be counted on to understand the gravity of their situation.

"Now dinner!" he exclaimed.

"Not just yet, it's hardly tea time silly boy. You wouldn't want to spoil your appetite. Soon we'll have a grand feast."

"But I'm hungry now."

"No, no, not yet. Here, want to play with the telescope again?"

Cat was very nearly at her wit's end, but there was no time for despair. Not when they'd made it so far already. She helped Morris climb onto the musty armchair she'd pushed to the boarded-up window, peering between the slats at the bustling town below. In the distance, the new tallport stretched high into the air, with airships of every shape and size gliding to and fro. If only they knew which they were looking for.

It had been three days since they'd arrived in the thick of an autumn storm. But last night the harvest moon had shone brightly overhead, the one night of the year when Cat knew where he would be.

And perhaps, she had been wrong.

Perhaps, he had decided not to attend the festival this year.

Perhaps, he had been captured or killed.

Perhaps…

Cat felt the sting of tears and focused on taking deep breaths as her brother snuggled into her warmth. She stroked his hair as her mind wandered into the forbidden territory of what to do if tomorrow came and the two of them were still friendless in a world that seemed to grow larger by the day.

But then…

"Cat, look! His hair's afire."

Startled out of her contemplation, she took the telescope and scanned the square for the red-haired man. He was walking down the street towards the merchants' bazaar, clad in the very same bright blue coat she remembered from the year before. It must be him. Her hands trembled as she handed the instrument back to her brother.

"There we are! I'm sure that's him, I'm sure of it. Quickly, gather your things."

The two of them picked up their meager possessions and

ran to the burnt-out stairwell. They slipped through the crowds, invisible. Two dirty children making their way through the streets. But by the time they reached the market, they'd lost track of their target. Cat's heart beat a little faster, they could not fail now! She turned into an alley with some boxes for cover, and tucked her brother behind them with their packs.

"I'll find him, I promise, and then I'll be right back. Remember what we practiced, quiet as a mouse," she said, placing a finger to her lips.

"Quiet as a mouse," he repeated solemnly.

She kissed him on the forehead and rejoined the throng. Unencumbered, she flitted from one store to the next, dashing from one end to the other, always peering through the forest of elbows for a glimpse of the bright blue coat until, at last, she found him by the milliners. He shook the man's hand as she crept closer to listen.

"That's the last of it then. It'll be a good year."

"Can I no entice ye to stay for a spot of dinner? Winnie's got a lovely stew on," said the merchant.

Cat's belly made its opinion on the matter loudly known.

"Regretfully, I must decline. We're due for another interception down the way and must leave post-haste. I'm heading back directly and Trick'll have my hide if he finds I've set us off course for any lesser reason than your wife's pot roast. The pilots still speak of it fondly."

The milliner guffawed and clapped the red-haired man on the back, "I'll send her your best, Captain. And ye can be sure she'll have one waiting for ye next harvest. Here, have a tart for the road."

Cat grinned. She was certain it was the right man now. But before she could approach, the Captain pocketed the treat and climbed into a waiting carriage with a wave. Her heart was gripped by ice, but as the horse passed her hiding spot at a short clip, she knew what she had to do.

She bolted toward the vehicle, boosting herself up using the footman's rest to cling to the side, then leapt up to grip the edge of the roof and propel her small frame through the window, landing in a heap on the floor.

"Ow," she said, rubbing her elbow.

"You may need to practice that a bit more," said the Captain Duke.

His right hand was tucked beneath his coat, some manner of concealed weaponry at the ready, Cat presumed. But at her glare, he removed a handkerchief instead and handed it to her. Blood was beginning to bead on the scrape on her arm, and she accepted it with thanks.

"Now that you have my attention, what might I do for you, little one?" he asked.

"Well, first we need to pick up my brother, and then we'll be going to your ship."

"Oh?"

"Yes. We'll be joining your crew, see?"

"Well. I hadn't expected this to be a recruiting mission, where is your brother?"

Cat could tell that he was humouring her. She could always tell when adults were telling fibs. She had him stop the carriage and sweetly asked for his hand before leading him firmly to the alley where Morris hid.

"It's safe! Quickly now!" she called.

The Captain tensed beside her, sensing a trap, but Cat gripped his sleeve tightly as her brother peered out from behind the crates. Immediately, his manner changed. He crouched in the dirt, carefully removing the tart from his pocket to offer it, hand outstretched, to the boy who grinned and tumbled out of his hiding place.

Two bites in, Morris beamed at Cat, "Quiet as a mouse!"

"Yes. Yes, you did very, very well."

The Captain was quiet as he watched their exchange, but Cat turned to him, determined. "We'll be going to your ship now."

"Tell me your name."

"Catherine Mary Margaret Waugh."

"Ah, little Cat. I thought I recognized you. You're a hand taller than last harvest. How old now? Eight?"

"Nine. And Morris will be three soon. He's hardly a bother, you'll see. I'll take care of him, he won't be any trouble."

"Don't be afraid, I will not part the two of you. But Cat, I need to know: Where is your father?"

He spoke the last word softly, as though he already knew the answer. Cat tried to reply in a steady voice, but felt as though she'd had the breath knocked out of her.

"They came for him. Three weeks ago. He said to warn you."

Cat felt her lower lip tremble, but she could feel Morris' stare and knew she must be brave as she fought for composure. The Captain looked her in the eyes as he rested a hand on her shoulder.

"You've done us a great service, little Cat."

He said nothing more, but picked up her brother with one arm and offered his other hand to her. Cat took a shaky breath, lifted her chin, and picked up their belongings before slipping her small hand into his.

They took the carriage to the tallport where the Captain boosted her brother onto his shoulders and led them up and up and up the spiral stair to a sleek and beautiful airship. A frowning man stormed onto the deck as soon as they had boarded.

"Now Captain, if I find out you've been to dinner at Winnie's without the rest of us–"

He stopped at the sight of the Captain Duke, blue coat flapping in the wind, a toddler clinging to his hair and a small girl standing at his side.

"Change course, Trick. We're being led into a trap. I'll explain later, but I think we may find time to pass by the Haven instead," he said, leading them toward the mess hall.

"But, Captain–"

"Oh, and I seem to have found us some new pilots. Meet Cat," said the Captain Duke, nodding in her direction, "and Mouse."

To be continued...

Sign up for the monthly **Airmail** newsletter for the latest news, appearances and bonus content for the Tales of the Captain Duke!

rebeccadiem.com/airmail-registration/

Author's Note

Once upon a time, an author was dreaming a steampunk dream of gadgets and gears and mad genius professors with clockwork limbs.

But she began to wonder: why does the Professor invent her inventions? What inspired her innovations at the forefront of this fictional technological boom?

And a story began to form. A child surrounded by books, living a thousand lives beyond the walls of her home. A young woman who saw opportunities in a way no one else could. A professor who made a practice of dismantling the limitations placed upon her work.

Professor Georgina Jameson Sewell is one of my favourite creations (named for Jamie and Georgina, who bought the 99th and 100th book sold at my first Fan Expo Canada in 2015), and she captures so much of the spirit of innovation I wanted to convey in this series.

The universe of the Tales of the Captain Duke is built on the idea that it's possible to twist the fabric of history and see our world in a different light. Steampunk disrupts our assumptions and opens us to the question: what if…?

What if there was a college built for female scholarship in the Victorian era, founded by Mary Somerville and funded by the heirs of Ada Lovelace?

What if the social model of disability was developed a hundred years earlier and prompted the kind of technological advances that would eradicate many injustices of the 20th century?

What if a band of airship pirates could challenge assumptions about mental health and identity, with powerful bonds of friendship?

These are the things I get to play with between the lines.

On a more historical note, one of my very early drafts for the series had the connection to Princess Beatrice and the Isle of Wight. Queen Victoria's youngest child was married to Prince Henry of Battenberg on July 23, 1885, almost a year to the day before Clara became the stowaway debutante. Their first child, Alexander, was born in November 1886. The Royal Family spent many summers on the Isle at Osborne House. Beatrice eventually married at a nearby church, and later retired to a private residence on the grounds of the estate.

Another detail is an essential feature of the town of Reading – Huntley & Palmers biscuits, a major economic driver of the region. Their biscuits were shipped all over the world in their distinctive tins. I liked the idea that Emily Palmer might have been a contemporary of Professor Sewell.

I have another secret.

I was reading *Orlando* by Virginia Woolf when I began to write the Tales of the Captain Duke. It's one of those gorgeous books that stays with you long after you turn the final page. The protagonist, Orlando, has a lover named 'Marmaduke Bonthrop Shelmerdine, Esquire,' and describes in detail his many nicknames, dependent on her mood:

'Tell me, Mar,' she would say (and here it must be explained, that when she called him by the first syllable of his first name, she was in a dreamy, amorous, acquiescent mood, domestic, languid a little, as if spiced logs were burning, and it was evening, yet not time to dress, and a thought wet perhaps outside, enough to make the leaves glisten, but a nightingale might be singing even so among the azaleas, two or three dogs barking at distant farms, a cock crowing — all of which the reader should imagine in her voice).

– Woolf, *Orlando,* Chp. 5

And that, Reader, is how our Captain found his name.

– Rebecca Diem
August 2016

Acknowledgements

It's been quite the year. I had no idea there would be so many of you when I started to publish my stories, and I'm thrilled to have the opportunity to share this one with you as well.

My first thanks are to you. For every tweet of encouragement, every comment and review, every time you shared my books with friends and family.

Thank you again to my editor, Arden Dier, whose thoughtful and merciless advice is responsible for countless improvements on my initial drafts.

Thank you to my beta readers, Lori Steuart and Paola Loriggio, for always being there to listen while I untangled a tricky bit of plot.

Thank you to Stevie Mikayne, for believing I could do it and keeping me sane while I did.

Thank you to Steve Armstrong for designing the cover and always finding the perfect portholes.

Thank you to Sarah Dier-McComb for the beautiful cover art. And I promise, here, in writing, that the next one will be a beach scene.

Thank you to the staff of the late, great Dark Horse Queen West, the eternal Bean Cellar, and my newest love, the Early Bird Espresso Bar. Finding myself bereft of a writing spot has made me treasure my favourites all the more.

Thank you to Brooklyn Marx for being such a powerful voice in our world and ensuring that Professor Sewell would be one in hers.

Thank you to the Toronto Steampunk Society for your support and inspiration. I couldn't ask for a better crew.

Thank you to my geek girl squad, who always get it, even when I can't even. ❤

And finally, to my family. These books are a collective effort, and I couldn't do it without your endless love and enthusiasm. Thank you.

– Rebecca Diem
August 2016

Photo: Britney Townsend

Rebecca Diem is a writer, music lover and nerd. She is the author of the indie steampunk series Tales of the Captain Duke, following the adventures of a defiant young aristocrat who saves a band of airship pirates from certain peril and talks her way into joining their crew.

An avid bookworm, Rebecca was honoured to receive a 'Nose in a Book' award from her elementary school librarian, and has a dedicated To Be Read shelf in her growing library. Somewhere between reading Virginia Woolf and Neil Gaiman she began to write her own stories.

Rebecca now calls Toronto home and is on a never-ending quest to find the perfect café and writing spot.

Web: rebeccadiem.com
Email: rebeccadiemauthor@gmail.com
Facebook: RebeccaDiemAuthor
Twitter/Instagram: @kthnxbex

Thank you so much for supporting my work.
Please share, rate and review!